Read What O

$\mathscr{Dark}$ LIGHT

"The Dark Light is creative, sexy, and well written. Dorian is one hot leading man and Jared...well, he had me at hello. S.L. Jennings left me wanting more!!!"
— **Janine** via Amazon

"I finished this book in one day. Just couldn't put it down. I loved how all the characters came to life... Its very well written and the story just pulled me immediately..."
— **Thuy** via Amazon

"A Great read! A definite page turner, excitement from start to finish with steamy scenes that got your pores open!"
— **Aisha Byrd** via Amazon

"Very intriguing! Not your typical romance. I love the mystery, the ongoing mix of emotions. I was unable to put this book down! I can't wait to read book two! I'm dying to know what's next."
— **Brandi "Brandi"** via Amazon

"I have to say that I LOVED this book! It keeps you guessing right up til the last page! Couldn't put it down! This one is a MUST read!!!"
— **Barbara Miller** via Amazon

OTHER TITLES BY S.L. JENNINGS

The Dark Light Series

Dark Light
The Dark Prince

Contemporary Romance

Fear of Falling

NIKOLAI

A *Dark* LIGHT NOVELLA

S.L. JENNINGS

Copyright © 2013 Syreeta L. Jennings
Book cover by Steph's Cover Design
Photography by Olga Martzoukou Photography
Model: Kyriakos Kanoulas
eBook Formatting by Danielle Blanchard
Paperback Interior Design by JT Formatting

www.facebook.com/**authorsljennings**

Printed in the United States of America
Library of Congress Cataloging-in-Publication Data

First Edition: December 2013

ISBN-13: 978-1494428013
ISBN-10: 1494428016

1. NIKOLAI (A Dark Light Series Novella)—Fiction
2. Fiction—Contemporary Romance
3. Fiction—New Adult & College

FOR PATTY

ONE

NEW ORLEANS, 1990S

So...close.

The stench of bourbon, cheap perfume and sex fill my nostrils, creating a heady cocktail of hedonism that takes me higher than I already am. Melodic sounds of live jazz resonate from Bourbon Street and meld with moans of raucous passion nearby. The eroticism of hearing someone else's pleasure, imagining the slick feel of damp skin against skin arouses me further, pushing me into oblivion. I let my head fall back and close my eyes, sucking in a breath through my teeth.

I'm close, but not close enough. Never close enough to feel ... whole. Complete. Full.

I'm not kidding myself. I know I'll never be satisfied. I'll always want more. More wealth. More power. More women. And while I have more of each than any one man should, it's not enough. It's never enough. The hunger is real. Deep. Overwhelming. Consuming me from the inside out.

I lift my heavy head and slowly peel open my eyes, gazing down at a crown of blonde, wavy locks bobbing up and down in my lap. I force myself to abandon all thought and just focus on the waves of sensation coursing through my body. Prickly white heat crawls up my legs and floods my veins before sinking into the heaviness between my thighs.

This ... I can do. This ... is easy.

Over and over again, my cock disappears into her wet mouth. Pink lips slide over the rigid, smooth skin, taking me deeper with every stroke. The swollen tip hits the back of her throat and she

1

doesn't even flinch. No gag reflex. Shit. This one is good. I think I'll keep her.

"Look at me, pretty girl," I tell her, gently grabbing a handful of her sunkissed hair. She complies with wide, eager eyes, but doesn't stall her movements. "That's right. Just like that. Take all of me. Deeper. I want to feel those sweet lips all over me."

She does as she's told with enthusiasm, desperate for my approval. She knows I'm *somebody*. Somebody important. Somebody that could potentially change her shitty existence. And I intend to, just not the way she's hoping.

Minutes tick by as I watch her suck me off with determination, growing more impatient, begging for my climax with her piercing gaze. She's giving me her all, pulling out all the tricks, fondling every erogenous zone known to man. An arrogant smirk plays on my lips before I put her out of her misery.

"You can stop now. Come," I say, patting my lap. She's only too willing to slide her thong clad ass on my thigh, thrusting her full, naked breasts in my face. I pluck a pink nipple before rolling the bud between my fingers, giving it a tug. She moans her pleasure and begins kissing my neck.

"Oooh, that feels good. Take me, please. I'm so hot for you. I want that big cock inside me." She trails wet kisses from my neck to my jaw. Wet heat seeps from her pussy and onto my slacks. Fuck. Just what I need - cum stains all over my Armani.

I shake my head. "No, baby." I caress her other breast to cushion the blow.

"But you didn't come. Let me make you come. I promise you; it'll feel real good. Please, baby. I'll do you right."

Again, I shake my head. "I don't come."

"Huh?" She lifts her head to access my expression. I look back at her with ice cold, blue eyes, devoid of even a trace of humor. "You don't come?"

"No. Never."

She flicks out her tongue and runs it along her bottom lip before donning an arrogant smile. "Well, you just haven't felt how good my pussy is."

My softening cock marginally jolts back to life with the feel of her warm, delicate hand wrapped around it. Her lips advance towards mine, causing me to raise a palm to halt her advances. I stifle a chuckle when her face crashes into my hand.

"And I don't kiss on the mouth."

Letting out an aggravated breath, she rolls her eyes. "Well... what *do* you do?"

"With you? Nothing. Not a goddamn thing."

"Nothing?" she spits indignantly. "Well, why the fuck am I here? So what...I'm good enough to suck you off, but not good enough to fuck?"

Growing bored with the annoyingly shrill sound of her voice, I stand faster than she can comprehend, and she tumbles onto the floor with a loud thud. I stuff myself back into my slacks and gaze down at the pathetic sack of flesh and bone covered only in a strip of black satin.

"Exactly. I don't fuck the talent."

Three raps on the door slice into the tension and Varshaun, my best friend and right hand, enters. "You called?"

I nod. "Take this one to Nadia." I crouch down to her level on the floor and run a hand through her blonde hair. Initially, she recoils but instantly relaxes under my touch, her gaze locked onto my icy blue irises. Bringing a coiled lock to my nose, I inhale the scent of her: earth, foliage and sunlight. Euphoria invades my lungs before spreading throughout my chest and abdomen. I close my eyes for a moment and savor it, letting it warm my cold, desolate soul. If only it were this simple. If only *this* was enough.

Dropping the lock of hair, I run a finger along her bottom lip. "We'll call her...Sunshine."

Before she can blink, she's airborne, and Varshaun is pulling her from the room. She looks as if she is on the brink of tears at the loss of my soothing touch.

"Wha…what? What are you doing? Where are you taking me? Sunshine?" she stammers, panic contorting her soft features. "What the fuck? That's not my name!"

In an instant, I'm in her face, roughly grasping her chin so she has no choice but to see the rage painted on my face. Her eyes widen with horror at the sight of me. *The real me.* There is no exotic beauty here. No trace of the carnal attraction that made her knees weak just minutes before. Only evil. Violence. Disgust.

"I. Don't. Give. A. *Fuck.* Your name is whatever I say it is. Do you understand, Sunshine? Can your pretty little head grasp that?"

"Yes…Yes…" she rasps with quivering lips. Lips that were wrapped around my hardness just minutes ago. Lips that could probably suck the paint off the walls.

"Yes, what?" I ask with a raised brow.

"Yes, Master."

"Good girl," I nod with a sinister grin. I pat her cheek before releasing her from my grip, composing myself as I straighten my suit jacket.

They're all nameless. Just faces. Lips, tongues, hands. Warm, wetness dripping with honey to stave off the hunger for *more*. More of what? I'm not sure.

Varshaun reappears in the doorway minutes later, a hint of alarm sparking his crystal blue eyes and making the contrast to his bronze skin even more startling. "We have a situation."

I take a moment to listen to the scene two floors below before exhaling my annoyance. Another one in need of a harsh reminder of who's in charge here. Of who *owns* them.

Females are so fucking temperamental. But, shit, they feel good. Plus, they make me a lot of money. Not that I need it.

"Well? Take care of it. Surely you can handle a simple, little woman."

Varshaun shakes his head. "This is no ordinary woman. She's … different."

My eyebrows rise marginally as I make my way to the en suite bar for a drink. The bourbon goes down smooth, and I refill my glass, downing that as well. I need to escape. To forget what I am. *Who* I am. And what I crave to do. *Will* do, again and again.

Most see me as cold and callous. Vile. Murderous. And they're right. But truth be told, I'm a conflicted motherfucker. I believe we all are, on some level. Some of us just can't afford the hassle of having a conscience. It's not good for business.

"Different," I murmur to myself. I turn to face Varshaun who still appears unsettled. "Something on your mind, old friend?"

He shakes his head, causing his long, black hair to sway. "I can't quite put my finger on it …"

I nod, hearing his thoughts. His apprehension. Yes, something's bothering him. Varshaun is not easily shaken, which is why I keep him close to me. I understand that kind of emotional detachment; it's the norm for me. His mental discord piques my interest. Not much rattles him. This has to be good, and I'm due for a little fun.

"Very well," I smirk, making my way across the room. "Let's see her."

I scent the air as we make our way towards the scene two stories below. Lust, greed, vanity and every other deadly sin in spades. Humans are weak. You tell them to stay away. You tell them not to touch the flame because it will burn.yet they still come to sate their licentious needs, getting off on the forbidden fruit dangled in front of their dumbstruck faces. They know it's wrong; they know that bright red apple is rotten to the core, festered with maggots and disease. But they want it. And I give it to them. I'd be a fool not to.

Fucking humans.

A few of the unoccupied girls stand in the doorways of their private rooms dressed in no more than lingerie, batting their false eyelashes in hopes that one of us will pay them a visit. I don't deny my men their carnal desires, but there is nothing in this house that will satisfy the magnitude of our craving. Not without consequence. And those consequences can get … messy. I don't do messy.

We enter the great room where three more of my men are

huddled around a small, dark dressed figure. Her screams are muffled but I can clearly detect her terror. The closer I get, the more aggravated I grow. We never take them against their will. They have to want this. They have to *feel* this. Sexual slavery just isn't my thing.

Sensing my presence, the men step aside to give me access to the situation. As I make my way through the barrier of their bodies, I freeze.

This…*girl*. This human girl, is all soft, smooth skin, long, dark tresses, and the most startlingly amber colored eyes I have ever seen in all my decades on this earth. Her body is petite and delicate, though she has a fiery strength in her that virtually pushes me like a force field, battling my solid frame with an unseen current.

I let my eyes find hers, but she quickly turns her head, refusing to meet my gaze. Ah, she knows. Either that or she's afraid. Good. She damn well should be. I, however, know fear does not power this girl. She is brave. Bold. And that tempts the fuck outta me. Every cell in my body hums and expands before nearly bursting with sensation. I can almost feel her soft, fragile skin under my eager fingertips. Smell her subtle scent of wildflowers and brown sugar. Taste the sweetness of her undiluted essence sizzling on my tongue.

"What do we have here?" I ask no one in particular, as I move closer to the girl. Her glassy eyes widen at the sight of my advance. Her fear is thick and palpable, but so is her strength. I am just much stronger. My resolve, however, may be another story.

I reach over to remove the gag from her mouth, careful not to graze her milky white skin, though I am aching to touch her. Her lips are cherry red and swollen, lush and waiting to be worshipped. Her reddened, puffy eyes look up at me in disgust. Hatred. Terror. She tries to extinguish it, but her petty mortal emotions give her away. It's the eyes. The eyes never lie. They are swimming with her truth, telling the tales she struggles to conceal.

Her full lips tighten into a grimace. "Get away from me, you piece of shit." Her broken voice is raspy and thick with unshed anguish. The sound sends an unfamiliar pang of discord to my chest.

"Why are you here, pretty girl?" I ask soothingly. I step forward and fondle a dark brown curl, breathing in her sweet scent.

She tries to jerk away from my touch, but she is bound. Not by rope or twine, but by power. Something you cannot see, something not entirely tangible, but she knows it's there, knows it's *real*. It lives in her as well.

We are both birthed into faith - unshakable belief of things beyond all logic and understanding. She knows deep inside that legends are truth. She knows that monsters are real. She can see me just as well as I can see her.

"Fuck you," she spews as she struggles against the invisible restraints. The corner of my mouth curls and I blink slowly. She's so … potent it nearly intoxicates me. I want more.

I turn to Varshaun and cock a brow. He takes a moment to read my unspoken question. "She was given to us. An unsettled debt that got… complicated. But, I agreed to take the girl in exchange for leniency."

"Since when do we accept whores as payment?" I grimace, turning my attention to her supple curves. Shapely thighs extend into round hips before cinching into a narrow waist. My mouth waters as I imagine how soft and warm she would feel beneath me. How those thighs would tighten and quiver while wrapped around my waist.

"I'm not a whore, asshole. Now let me go!" she demands, still unable to give up her futile struggle. I laugh, admiring her determination. And she's right - I am an asshole. A damn good one too. I'm nothing if not a perfectionist.

I stroke the luminescent skin of her cheek lightly, feeling the burn underneath my fingertips. It's unpleasant but not unbearable enough to make me stop touching her. The feel of her skin against mine sends a jolt of electricity through my frame, stirring my senses from decades of numbness and detachment. This girl is different, indeed. Special. And dangerous.

I want her badly. So much so that I'm willing to break my own rules, and that fact fucks with me.

"Don't you fucking touch me," she seethes in a harsh whisper. "I know what you are."

The conviction in her voice causes me to drop my hand, and I frown. She may be able to feel my power, even see it radiating around me, but there's no way she could know exactly *what* I am. She's human. Stupid. Weak. Ignorant. She is ultimately a flea compared to me. We're more than cautious about protecting our identities, and those who happen to learn our secret are eliminated without question.

I peg her with an icy glare. "Who sold you, pretty girl?" The bite in my voice doesn't match the tenderness of my words.

Those big eyes are instantly assaulted with a flash flood of tears and her succulent mouth goes slack. She turns her head and furiously bats her wet lashes in an attempt to hide the pain that so obviously haunts her. I want to grasp her cheeks and make her look at me. I want to lick every salty tear that slides down from those mesmerizing eyes. I want to drink her in, feel her inside of me. *Be* inside of her.

"Who?" I repeat, softening my tone.

I watch her slender throat as she swallows laboriously. "My father," she manages to choke out through a rogue sob. "And he didn't sell me. I came on my own accord. To save his life."

I nod, though I don't quite understand her depth of devotion. It's a modern day Beauty & the Beast. This brave, human girl has sacrificed her life in order to save another. She's thrust herself into darkness and danger, completely blind to the sheer evil that lies in this room alone. Yet, she's done the unthinkable, only to save a sloppy drunk with a gambling problem.

This beautiful girl has selflessly put her life in the hands of a villainous monster. In *my* hands.

I've never felt that magnitude of loyalty for anyone … except my brother. But he's gone, abandoning me to figure all this shit out on my own. Dorian was the good one. The smart one. The one that kept me from fucking up everything our family has built and stood for. The only one that ever understood me and loved me anyway. Yet, he's turned his back on us. On *me*. The one person that needed him the most.

I flex my hands into fists as tension settles in my joints. Why the fuck does this shit still bother me? How can I possibly give a damn about him? Once the years turned into decades, I merely stopped counting. I knew he would never come back. And can I really blame him? After what our father did to him? Would I have stayed and pledged my allegiance to the man that made it his personal mission to turn my life into rot and ruin?

I want to bury this shit. I want to erase all the confusion and anger that has haunted me my entire life. Never good enough… always the black sheep. I need to find a substitute for the turmoil brewing inside my hollow chest, bubbling over until it feels like acid singing my throat. I want to end it all and forget what I am. *Who* I am.

"I know …" a sweet voice whispers, a soothing balm to my black, tormented soul. I look up and my blue eyes collide with warm, molten honey. "I know," she whispers again.

I swallow down my sudden upheaval and plaster on a cool smile. "What do you know, darling?"

Her full, bottom lip trembles, and she quickly tucks it away between her teeth. "I know who you are."

I take a step towards her, generously scenting the space between us, getting high off the mix of fear and arousal. "Everybody knows who I am." Shit, at least they think they do.

Her gaze never falters. Not even a hint of uncertainty as those haunting eyes slice right into me. She merely watches as I bleed out onto the marble floor. "But do they know *what* you are?"

I freeze where I stand. Not because I've been exposed; hell, inside these four walls, there's no question of my identity. But what really strips me bare, making it impossible to hide from the truth I so desperately want to escape, is the almost question on those crimson lips. The same question that has been permanently burned inside my skull.

Do I *know what I am?*

I turn my gaze away, refusing to let her see what lies beneath. I don't care what she thinks of me. She's wrong. She's a stupid whore who wouldn't know the damn truth if it bent her over and fucked her seven ways from Sunday.

"Varshaun," I bark, my voice raw and harsh. "Take the girl to Nadia; get her cleaned up. Then place her in my chambers."

I need a distraction. Something to stifle any inklings of guilt or empathy. Avoidance. Denial. Escapism. It's what I'm good at. It's what I create for the weak and perverse. I provide a place of fantasy and desire, allowing them to indulge in the taboo without fear of exposure or judgment.

We're all monsters here. And I'm the most fucked up of them all.

Blocking out the sounds of struggle below, I climb the stairs up to my room before stopping mid step. "And get ready," I demand over the commotion, perched high above the fray of debauchery and hedonism. "We're going out."

TWO

It's all a blur.

Loud music. Alcohol. Drugs. They're all necessary evils. All part of my plan.

It's easy to forget when you don't remember.

We stumble up to my room, our hysterical laughter echoing throughout the vast house. Nobody pays us any attention. They're all too caught up in their own immorality to give a fuck about ours. Besides, I make no qualms about what I want. I not only live up to my reputation, I embrace it with open arms.

The blonde on my left sucks my neck while my hand snakes up her dress. The brunette on my right works at the buttons of my slacks as I pull down her top to expose a swollen breast. In the next instant, her pebbled nipple is in my mouth, between my teeth, as my tongue elicits indecent sounds. My hand finds the slick, wet flesh between the blonde's legs, and her moans compete with her friend's. They grind against me, clawing at my hair, my back, my dick ... battling for climax. I feel them both throbbing, both trembling with want. With *need*. And I plan to give them what they desire. But first, I want to play.

I toss them both on the bed and gaze down at their panting bodies with a sly grin. They're both nameless, just like the rest of them. I don't care. They're *open* to me, their thoughts and emotions completely unguarded. This'll be fun.

"Undress," I order. Without hesitation, the girls slip off the remainder of their garments, their eyes locked on mine the entire time. *That's right ... eyes on me.*

They spread their naked bodies out for me to admire, their smooth, supple skin calling out to be caressed. The scent of arousal is heavy and thick in the air. I can nearly taste them; it's so palpable. Sweet, salty, tangy. My mouth waters in expectation.

"Come. Let us help you out of those clothes," the brunette says, her arm outstretched.

I shake my head. "Not yet. Soon. But first, I want you two to kiss."

Again, without hesitation, the girls comply, their soft, sweet lips gently touching. They giggle against each other's mouths, their lips working together until their breaths quicken, and their pink tongues intertwine hungrily. They touch each other, their arousal building and building until they both are whimpering for release. Not yet. Not until I've had my fill.

They break apart, panting, whining and still petting the other's soft, sensitive skin.

"Good," I smile. I lock my gaze on the blonde. "Suck her tits."

She takes the round globes into her small palms and runs her thumbs along the nipples. Through her long lashes, Blondie looks at her friend before sweeping her gaze to me. Then she takes the taut skin into her mouth and sucks, gently pulling as she keeps her hooded eyes locked onto mine.

Laughter has ceased. Nothing can be heard but the erotic sounds of uninhibited pleasure. I caress their smooth, flawless skin as they move against each other, pure bliss harmonizing with the thrill of dark fantasy.

They don't question what they feel. They don't hesitate nor do they resist. They let their carnal instincts guide them - let *me* guide them. I am their teacher. Their leader. Their god. And they want nothing more than to please and worship me.

Some time later, when their wants have exploded into need, I am behind the brunette, entering her while her face is buried between the blonde's legs. She moans against her sex, and they both cry out. Deeper I plunge, harder, faster. I let the wet warmth envelop me, let it draw out the fire that burns me from within, scorching my nerve endings until all I can do is feel. Every taut muscle in my body tightens and pulses, yet I don't stop, only pausing to flip her over in a blur of motion that she doesn't even register with her until I am thrusting into her again.

I go for hours, taking each of them, exhausting them beyond their limits. And just when they feel like their bodies may implode with overwhelming sensation, I take them again, until they are too spent to move and too hoarse to even moan.

I lie on the bed, staring up at the ceiling, and imagine the lullaby of their heavy breathing rocking me to sleep. But I know it's futile; sleep never comes. It never takes me away from this. From me.

Grabbing my discarded slacks, I ease them on and make my way over to the bar. The bourbon goes down like liquid fire, and I exhale the flames.

"Enjoy the show?" I say aloud, pouring another.

No answer. I don't expect one anyway.

"You know, you could do well. Especially if you're willing to do some girl on girl." I turn towards the shadowed edge of the room and smile. "Customers like that shit."

"You make me sick," a broken mumble retorts. "Fuck you."

"Sorry, baby," I chuckle, walking towards the voice. "But I don't fuck the merchandise. But who knows … maybe you'll be my exception. If you're a good girl, that is."

I stand in the darkest corner of the room, shrouded in the shadows, in front of her. The girl. The amber eyed girl with a death wish is cowered between a dresser and an armchair, desperately trying to melt into the wall to escape. But she can't. She couldn't leave even if her miserable little life depended on it. She's been spelled to remain within the mansion's four walls.

"I'm not a whore, you disgusting piece of shit," she whispers angrily.

"Of course you aren't." I crouch down to her level, drink in hand. I extend the glass to her, but she recoils as if I've offered her a cup full of blood. "But, as you know, I house whores here. No one lives here for free."

Her eyes shine with tears and she quickly turns her head so I can't witness their escape. My hand twitches, longing to reach out and follow the trail of moisture down her cheek. Instead, I down my drink to numb the urge.

"Why?" she asks suddenly.

I shrug. "Prostitution is one of the oldest forms of employment. Sex will always be in demand."

"No…why do *you* do it? Why do you take innocent girls and degrade them to nothing more than waste receptacles? Don't you have any guilt at all? Don't you even feel bad for being such a pathetic waste of space?"

I smile against the irritation. "First off, I don't *take* anyone. The women employed here are here at their own choosing. And in case you didn't realize, none are hurting. They have the finest clothing, are treated to regular salon and spa visits, and have round the clock protection. Trust me, they could be doing a lot worse, and before me, most of them were. And to answer your second question … no. I don't have any guilt. Guilt is for the weak and emotional. To harbor guilt, you must care. And I don't give a fuck about a goddamn thing."

She shakes her head and quirks a sardonic smile. "Wow. And here I thought princes were supposed to be more dignified."

I nearly jump out of my fucking skin. *Prince.* She knows. Fuck, she knows …

"And here I thought whores were supposed to be more agreeable," I retort with a straight face, expertly masking my panic.

"I. Am. Not. A. Whore!" she growls. The girls sleeping just feet away stir, yet don't wake.

I lift an amused brow. "Is that right? Well, what do you plan to do for me? You know the nature of my business; you know there is a debt to be settled. How do you plan to pay off your father's balance?"

Her lip trembles and she bites down on it hard enough to turn it from crimson to white. She looks away, blinking away stubborn tears and desperately trying to hide her fear from me. I know I have caused that fear, and I want to see it. I crave it - those raw, human emotions. I want her tears, but then again, a part of me doesn't want to make her cry.

See? Conflicted motherfucker.

"Whatever you want," she finally whispers, turning her gaze back to me. Though she most likely cannot see my face, her expression is stoic and certain. Brave. "Whatever you want me to do."

I nod passively although I'm shocked as shit at what she has just agreed to. And maybe a little disappointed. Maybe I wanted her to fight me. Maybe I wanted her to refuse because she believes it is disgusting and wrong. Not wholeheartedly accept it. No sane, self-respecting girl would sign up for this shit.

I run a hand through my hair and pull it in unexplainable anger. This girl has no business in a brothel, yet here she is, and I'm too fucking stubborn to do anything about it. And the fact that I want to - shit, I want to excuse her from any debt her pathetic excuse for a father has bequeathed upon her – seriously fucks with me.

"Right. Well, we should begin your audition immediately," I say flatly. I stand upright and begin to unfasten my slacks.

"Wha … what? What are you doing?" Her eyes are wide with horror as she catches a glimpse of the patch of black hair peeking out from my loosened pants.

"What do you think I'm doing? I can't sell what I don't sample. Now I can understand you may be reluctant to suck me off so I'll make an exception just this once." Faster than she can see, still hidden by the dark of night, I crouch before her. "I'll let you fuck me, pretty girl. Is that what you want? After seeing me fuck those other girls? After making them moan and scream my name? You want that too, don't you? You want me deep inside you just as I was deep inside of them."

When I reach for the strap of the silk nightgown that Nadia dressed her in, I can feel her trembling beneath my fingertips. She whimpers the second my skin touches hers, the slight burn traveling from my fingers and sinking deep in my gut.

"No," she says through a broken sob. "Please, don't do this."

"What? Would you rather undress yourself?" I sneer angrily, clutching the delicate fabric. "Don't get stage fright on me now. You're the one who signed up for this."

"Bu-but...I can't. I can't do this. Stop, please."

I draw my hand back and place it at my side, balling it into a tight fist. As badly as I want to touch her, as much as I crave her feelings of raw terror, I don't want this. No. Not like this.

"Isn't this what you want?" I ask through clenched teeth. "Isn't this what you came here for?"

"Yes!" she cries. "But I - I...I can't."

"You can't? You can't what? What kind of whore can't fuck?" I roar. The girls behind us on the bed begin to stir, but I quickly put them down again with a quick flick of my wrist. I don't even care about being inconspicuous. All I can focus on are the next words that escape those full, red lips.

"The kind of whore that's a virgin!" she yells, matching my fury. Her chest heaves rapidly, causing her nostrils to flare with every labored breath.

I reel back, putting more than a foot between us as if she's revealed some communicable disease rather than her virtue. She's a virgin, yet she's banished herself to a life of shame and debasement. Damned herself to live with a monster. Even I can't wrap my head around it, and I'm the king of mind-fucks.

I open my mouth to voice my initial reaction, cold pressure building behind my eyes. I flex my fists, calming the frigid storm racing in my veins. "A virgin? You're a fucking virgin? What the hell am I supposed to do with *that?*"

She doesn't answer. Instead, she wipes her dampened face with the back of her hand, pinning me with a heated glare. We sit in heavy silence, the weight of her words feeling like boulders pressed down on my shoulders. I'm a sick bastard - I've never hidden that fact - but could I really destroy this girl and take her most sacred gift, selling it to the highest bidder? Do I really have the capacity for that type of evil?

I shake my head, answering my own question. I am that evil. I am that selfish. My soul was damned the moment I was birthed. But the rest of me? Undecided. And no matter how hard I try to accept the path of depravity that has been paved in bone and blood with my birthright, something in me refuses to embrace it. It fights against it, thrashing against my nature, ensuring that I am in a constant state of doubt. Which is why I do what I do - why I fuck my feelings away. Why I numb it all with alcohol, drugs, anything to make it easier to play this role.

That's what makes me the despicable creature that I am. I know better. I know that what I am, what I do, is wrong. But I do it anyway. I do it because I can.

"You said you know who I am," I rasp through an unfamiliar tightness around my throat.

"I do." Certainty resonates in her unwavering voice.

"And...*what* I am?"

"Yes."

I nod. She doesn't have to say it. I can feel her truth. I can see it. Hell, I can smell it on her, the scent of her bloodline nearly making me dizzy. This is no ordinary girl. Human, but only just so. As if she was filled with something supernatural. Something powerful. Something like me.

I could easily make her forget. I could erase any trace of my identity from her mind. Shit, I could take away every memory she's ever had. But for some uncanny reason, I don't. Maybe for once, I don't want to be a stranger. Maybe I just want someone – anyone - to know *me.*

"What's your name, pretty girl?" I ask against my better judgment. Names signify familiarity. They're personal, and I don't do personal. I've never had the desire. Not until now.

She hesitates, and I imagine her having the same mental

struggle. The hollow space in my chest aches - another foreign feeling.

"Amelie," she finally whispers. And before she can regret disclosing the first intimate piece of herself to me, I lift a hand and softly sweep it across her forehead, sending her into a peaceful sleep.

"Nice to meet you, Amelie," I whisper, as I cradle her warm body just as she slumps forward, my lips so close to her skin, I can smell the sweetness of her essence. Brushing a lock of hair from her face, I gaze down at the purest, most beautiful being I have ever held in my arms. "I'm Niko."

Three

I stand at the foot of the bed, gazing down at the naked bodies twisted in rumpled satin sheets. Pale moonlight kisses their skin, making them appear ethereal, ghostlike even.

So beautiful. So soft. So weak.

I lean forward, propping a knee onto the mattress, and position myself between their sleeping forms. My fingers graze their soft skin, leaving a trail of goosebumps in their wake. I inhale their combined scents, picking up traces of alcohol, sweat and sex. And something else. Something *more*. It invades my lungs and bursts in my chest, sprouting tingling warmth in my extremities.

Magic.

Just a drop between the two, but it will do. These days, it's harder and harder to find more than that. In a willing donor, that is.

I lay down facing the brunette, my hands exploring the soft contours of her body. I brush her cheek with the back of my hand. She was stunning once - I can tell - but her indulgences have aged her. Her vices, her weaknesses, have not been kind to her. She'll die before her time, I'm certain of it.

"Wake," I whisper. Instantly, her eyes open, and once her pupils adjust to the dark, she smiles.

"Hey," she says, caressing my bare chest.

I give her a slight smile and cup her face between my hands. "Look at me."

She complies instantly, looking back at me with trusting, brown eyes. Eyes that will forget that they ever saw my face. They dilate within seconds and her body relaxes against mine. She's completely *open* to me - her thoughts, her actions... all mine. But most of all, her magic. The tiny trace concealed in her bloodline flows freely into my body as I inhale at the base of her neck. I moan and let my teeth graze her throat.

Fuck, it feels good. It always does, transcending any measure of human pleasure. Breathing is beyond feeling. Beyond physical sensation. It's complete and utter euphoria, exploding in every synapse. It's feeding your soul and making love to your spirit; it's life itself.

My dick twitches to life, and soon I am hot and hard against her thigh. "Touch me," I mutter, my mouth moving down her chest. She unleashes me and begins to stroke, only heightening the sheer bliss pumping through my veins. I squeeze my eyes tight and imagine it's someone else caressing me. Someone else kissing the side of my face as I lick a trail from her collarbone to her hardened nipple.

Amelie. It's as if the name is carried by a wisp of wildflower scented air.

I bury my face deeper into her skin, trying to lose myself … in myself. My desires, my secrets, my fears. They're all magnified times ten, drowning me in the once perfectly contained emotions that seep from the cracks of my broken soul.

I can feel the pull … the pull towards her. Beckoning me to relent and stop the charade. My whole fucking life is a charade, and I'm nothing but a puppet, dancing around like a fucking fool in hopes of some type of acceptance. Some sign that I'm more than a philandering piece of shit. More than a cold, ruthless killer.

More than my father.

"Wake," I growl against humid skin. Within seconds, another set of hands joins us, kneading my shoulders and back. The blonde kisses my neck as she moves her body into my line of vision, offering it to me. Roughly, I grab her waist and pull her to me, burying my face in her neck and chest. Her scent, her flavor, is subtly sweet, warm, but not warm enough. Not sweet enough. Not like her. Not like…

Amelie.

This time I pause, but only long enough to part her legs and sink into her without warning. She cries out from shock, pleasure, and even a bit of pain. I don't care. I don't give a fuck about anything right now. The brunette positions herself over the blonde's mouth, sating her own fiery need. She offers herself to me, and again, I take her. But her magic is waning. She's weak. And while her body seeks pleasure, her soul is slowly dying. She sags against me, trembling with the aftershocks of orgasm and fatigue. I push her aside, digging into the blonde's wet core with unrelenting strokes.

Just focus on this. Just this lustful act. Nothing else but this. Because it means nothing. She means nothing. And I feel...nothing.

I fuck her until she can't take anymore, breathing nearly every drop of life from her limp body. When I finally stop, I realize she's unconscious and eerily pale. Doesn't matter. I pull out of her and sit on the edge of the bed, tugging at my hair, wishing like hell it would help me forget. That it would take away that urge to go to her. I don't understand it - shit, I've never felt it before - but it's there. And, dammit, it's stronger than anything I have ever felt. Maybe even stronger than me.

Amelie. A soft whisper caresses my ears before floating into my body, sinking deep into my hollow chest.

That's the thing about names. Once you learn them, once they're burned into your skull, you're forever connected to that person. You know them. You wonder if they have family or friends that care for them. You wonder if they have dreams and aspirations they wish to achieve. Wonder if anyone would miss them if they suddenly disappeared. Names give way to guilt, and guilt is a useless motherfucker that has no business in my head.

But I know her name. And, *fuck me*, I want to know *her*.

Amelie.

A knock at the door causes me to flinch, although I'm expecting it. I always expect it. Nothing surprises me anymore … nothing until *her*.

"Enter," I rasp in a hoarse whisper, not bothering to look up to see who it is. I don't need to; I already know.

"Ready?" a deep, haunting voice asks. If he wasn't my cousin, even I would be a little spooked.

I lift my head, almost tensing at his bright red eyes and menacing sneer that showcases a mouthful of razor sharp teeth. Years ago, Cyrus was known for his adventurous, borderline suicidal, zest for life. He never backed down from a challenge, and at 6-foot-5, he didn't have to. He was a mountain of a beast and unstoppable when it came to the things he wanted.

That was before…before the accident. The accident that claimed his life and left us with mere seconds to decide his eternal fate. And when Dorian decided that he wasn't ready to say goodbye to our family, he turned him. Turned him into the monster that stood before me today. *A vampire.*

Cyrus, of course, was a proud man, and less than pleased with the decision. Living out his days as servant to the Dark was never his plan. He would rather have died. But when you live your life making enemies and not giving a damn who it affects, you cling to the ones you truly care for. Cyrus was one of those people. We had grown up together, and Dorian valued his presence in our life just as much as I did. We needed him. Letting him die wasn't an option.

"I'm done," is all I manage to say.

Cyrus nods before swiftly crossing the room. He stands at the foot of the bed, looking down at the ghostly pale, naked bodies strewn across it. He turns to me and narrows his startling, blood red eyes.

"What did you do?"

I shake my head and look at the floor. "Went a little too far. I don't know … I don't know what got into me."

He nods and jerks the blonde towards him by her ankle before slinging her virtually lifeless body over his shoulder. "I'll handle it." Then he does the same with the brunette, holding them both effortlessly as if they weigh next to nothing. He turns just as he hits the doorway, inhaling deeply through his mouth, no doubt tasting the air. Tasting fresh, live blood. He takes a step back into the room.

"And her?"

I force my eyes towards the dark corner of the bedroom, where Amelie's body is shrouded in shadowy night. She still sleeps peacefully on the carpeted floor. I've even placed a pillow under her head and covered her with a quilt.

What the fuck is wrong with me?

"Leave her."

Cyrus narrows his crimson eyes and frowns like he doesn't understand. But I match his glare; mine even more menacing and cold. It screams of hostility and the promise of violence. It dares him to challenge my authority.

"Very well," he mutters. Then he's gone, the soiled sheets the only reminder of my guests for the evening. I rip them from the bed and hastily replace them with fresh ones, determined to forget the lives that were so greedily taken tonight. I know those girls won't live. Cyrus will drain them and then dispose of their bodies. He'll clean up any evidence that they were even here. He's done it before for me, even for Dorian.

Amelie deserves better than that. Better than having the life sucked out of her soul before being drained of every drop of her blood. Better than being discarded in an abandoned alleyway, made to look like just another cracked-out Quarter whore with a syringe jabbed into her pale arm.

Still, I know that better is not *me*. I'm not the one to give it to her - I can't. *Better* is not in my nature. And feeling like this - so drawn to her, so completely vulnerable to my conflicted feelings - is so far out of my realm that I can't even comprehend it.

I don't fucking *get* it.

She's human. An inconsequential, human girl that is good for nothing more than fucking and breathing. She's disposable, just like the rest of them. I am Dark - a god amongst men. And she is nothing to me. I don't know her. I don't need her, and I don't want her.

Uncontrollable laughter rings in my ears. Hell, even the voices in my head know that I'm full of shit.

I mindlessly cleanse myself of the scent of sex and cheap perfume, determined to erase any trace of the past hours. I can't wash it all away though. The guilt, the shame remain. I can't run from my Achilles heel.

Before I know what I am doing, I am crouched beside Amelie's sleeping body. She breathes deeply, her body perfectly relaxed in slumber. So trusting. I trail a finger from her cheek to her collarbone, feeling the slight burn that lights my fingertip with tiny gold sparks. I saw it the first time I touched her, but concealed it from the rest of my men. They knew she was different, they just didn't know *how* different. And how devastating her eccentricity could be for our kind … and for me.

I know what she is, and she knows what I am. Because of this revelation, there's only one solution. Only one conclusion to this tragic tale that has only just begun.

I will kill her.

FOUR

Sunlight kisses her lips and caresses her cheeks, before warming her eyelids. I watch with rapt attention as the brilliant heat flushes her translucent skin before slowly parting. She blinks rapidly, then rubs her weary eyes with the back of her hand. Then, as lithe and graceful as a cat, she stretches her arms above her head and yawns, a raspy, sultry sound rumbling her throat.

"Well, good morning, love," I smirk, my voice as smooth as silk.

Shock pries open her tired eyes and she tries to scream, but fear has stolen her breath. It wouldn't matter. No one would hear her cries. Nor would they care.

"Whe … where am I?" she stammers.

I look on either side of us. "Well … this is what you'd call a bed. You know, some people like to sleep on them. Even fuck on them. I prefer the latter."

Amelie narrows her eyes and purses her full lips. "I know that. How did I get here? And what did you do to me?" Pulling the comforter up to her chin, she shifts to the edge of the bed.

"I obviously put you in bed - *my* bed. And I haven't done anything to you. Not yet, at least." I move closer to her, and watch as her eyes widen, taking in the sight of my bare chest. "And if I wanted to see what was under that nightie, believe me, you'd be naked and spread eagle right now. And if you're lucky, my tongue would be buried deep inside you." I tug at the covers just to rattle her further, and she doesn't disappoint. A slow smile spreads across my face.

"You're sick."

"I've been called worse," I shrug.

"You're a disgusting, perverted piece of shit."

"Worse than that, too."

Her bottom lip trembles and she quickly tucks it away between her teeth. "What do you want from me?"

I finger the delicate fabric of her satin nightgown. The image of me ripping it off her flashes in my head, and warmth sinks into my abdomen.

"For now…I want you to tell me who sent you."

Amelie turns to me and frowns as if I've just slapped her. "Who sent me?"

I smile. Not my usual panty wetting grin that makes chicks weak in the knees. No, I give her the one that lets her know how fucking crazy I can be. The one that tells her that I will rip her limb from limb just for the fuck of it. The one that shows her just how evil I truly am. *How Dark I am.* If she was unsure of what I am capable of before, there's no mistaking it now.

Amelie swallows, the annoyance in her expression wiped clean and replaced with inimitable fear. She sees me for what I am: a monster. Vile, disgusting, ruthless. The stuff nightmares are made of. And here she is, sharing a bed with the epitome of sin. Not even her innocence can save her.

"No one sent me," she states with unwavering conviction.

I move in closer, so close that I'm surrounded by her scent. So close that I can feel the heat of her body wash over me and count every one of her precious heartbeats.

"Oh?" I smirk with a raised brow. "No one sent you yet you just happen to know who I am? As if it's public knowledge?"

Desperation lights her eyes, the unusual color growing brighter, hotter. "I swear no one sent me."

Before she can take her next breath, I am on top of her, pinning her body underneath mine. She can't move. She can't speak. She can hardly think. All she feels is *me,* dominating the very air she rapidly breathes.

"Now, sweet girl, I'm going to ask you one more time before I rip that pretty little head off your shoulders. Who sent you?"

She shudders, her mouth agape in horror. I know what she sees when she looks at me. Eyes so cold that they're almost opaque. White, gleaming teeth that now appear as razor sharp fangs. Pale, ashen skin that speaks of old Voodoo legends told around the fire, warning children of the dangerous, evil creatures that thirst for their souls.

She sees me, and I allow her. Maybe for shock value, or maybe because I know she'll never survive long enough to confirm the legends of her people. But I let her take it all in … the nightmare that is me. The Dark One that needs to kill her … yet wants to own her.

"Please … I swear," she rasps through trembling lips. "No one. No one sent me."

I release a hiss between clenched teeth. "See, I don't believe you. Now you can either tell me the truth, or I will be forced to resort to more … carnal … forms of persuasion." I bring my face closer to hers, so close that we share the same breath. "And I really don't want to do that. Such a pity for that pretty face to go to waste."

Tears sprout at the corners of her eyes and slide down the sides of her face. I don't even try to resist; I can't. I lean forward and lick the salty moisture, tasting the mixture of her sweet skin and tears. When shudders rack her frame, I look down at her through my euphoric haze and smile. "You want me to torture it out of you, huh? You want me to pop that sweet little cherry and fuck you until the point of agony. Don't you? Because you are a little whore. You are all lying, scheming whores. Maybe I've been too lenient. Maybe you only respond to pain."

Her frightened eyes widen as my hand wraps around her slender neck, applying just enough pressure to let her know that I'm serious. She won't win this. There's no escape. I can and will kill her, no matter how badly I want her.

I close my eyes and suck in a breath. Fuck … the feeling of her body beneath mine sheathed only in thin satin, her scent so potent it's damn near palpable, the taste of her tears…

How can I resist her? How can I not want to rip her flimsy nightgown off her and sink into her for hours?

I shake the thoughts from my head and tighten my grip. "Tell me," I growl. I'm angry - with her for being so fucking enticing and with myself for being so weak. I can't let my father be right about me. I am a Skotos, goddammit. Mercy isn't even in my vocabulary.

"No one! I swear it! On my life!" she cries hoarsely, the pressure on her vocal cords restricting her screams.

"Then how? How do you know me? How the fuck do you know who I am?"

Her tears flow freely, wetting my hand and her hair. I squeeze harder. "Fucking tell me now or so help me-…"

"I dreamt of you!" she screeches brokenly. Even through the garble of tears, I hear her clearly. *Dreamt of me.* It's a trick - I know it is. But still, I release her neck and roll off her, huffing out frustration and … shame? No. Of course not.

"You dreamt of me?" I'm panting but not winded.

"Yes," she whispers, refusing to meet my gaze. Her hand flies up to her neck, and she winces.

"When?"

Look at me. Please. I need to see the truth.

Finally, Amelie turns her heated amber glare on me, fear and loathing still clouding the unusual irises. She hates me, and she should. But I can't help but feel … I don't know … conflicted about it. She swallows and fresh tears fill her eyes. Right about now, I hate myself too.

"Since I was young. Since I was just a little girl, I have dreamt of you every night."

"Bullshit," is all I can say in disbelief. But I see it - the truth in those mysterious eyes.

She shakes her head in disgust and looks away, focusing on some random spot on the wall. "I wish it were. Every day of my life, I have wished that I could close my eyes and not see your face. Not hear your voice. Not have you haunting me for 10 fucking years!"

Suddenly, she turns her head and I almost wince at the look of pure hatred and repugnance on her face. "Do you know what that's like? To have to see evil every single day? To have your nightmares replayed on a continuous loop? To be forced to know someone that makes you wish you had never been born? Because I do. I know you because I have to. Because I was cursed to in order to live. And you know what? I wish I would've died. How does that make you feel, *your majesty?* How do you feel knowing that I would rather be dead than have to see your face for one more day?"

Her words sting like a slap to the face, but I press for more. "Why do you have to?"

She turns away with a grimace as if tasting something foul. "When I was young, I fell ill. Doctors couldn't find the root of the infection. My parents were told that I only had days, maybe weeks, to live."

I move closer, hanging onto every word, every breath. She exhales and continues, although I can see the painful memory is a struggle to conjure. "My mother's family had certain beliefs that led them to believe I had been cursed. See, my mom denied their way of life. She didn't want that for me. Her name was Genevieve. Genevieve Laveau."

Laveau.

"Your mother is a witch," I hiss, my eyes lighting with blue fire. If there's one thing the Dark despise, it's unnatural magic. Magic that calls upon the dead and worships false deities, disrupting the balance of nature. Amelie and her mother are direct descendants of Marie Laveau, also known as the Voodoo Queen of New Orleans. We had exterminated most of the Voodoo garbage in the city over a century ago, but Laveau and her family had ways of evading us. And I've had one lying beside me this entire time. I should have known. I should have fucking known.

"No," Amelie whispers, shaking her head. "She wasn't. Maybe Voodoo was in her blood, but she never practiced. At least, not when I was around. Doesn't matter anyway - she's dead."

29

"She sacrificed her life to save yours," I say, trying to piece together the story.

"If only it were that easy." Amelie's voice is thick and strained with emotion. "One night, a woman came to me at my bedside in the middle of the night. I don't remember much, just that she was beautiful and kind. And that I felt oddly at peace with her presence. She was … like a dream or a ghost, but I wasn't afraid.

"She said that I would not die yet - that it was my destiny to do a great and remarkable thing. Something necessary that would aide in the safety of our world. I didn't understand then, and honestly, I still don't. I didn't stop her when she cupped my face and smiled down at me. Then…something crazy happened. I know it sounds insane, but she started, like, glowing in the dark. She was as bright as the sun - so bright that I thought it may blind me. And then, she was gone."

Amelie turns to me, her face blank and devoid of emotion. "That was the first night I saw your face in my dreams. The first time I ever saw pure evil."

I know that this is my chance. This is the time to cradle her delicate neck and squeeze it so hard that it shatters like glass underneath my fingertips. This girl is dangerous - more dangerous than I ever could imagine. If I don't kill her soon, she is sure to destroy me.

"And the woman?" I hear myself ask, ignoring the niggling voice in my head, telling me to put an end to this conversation, along with her life. "Do you know what she was?"

The rims of Amelie's irises spark with golden flames for a mere nanosecond, both taunting and answering me. "She was goodness. Warmth. Mercy. She was the complete opposite of everything that is you."

"Light," we both whisper in unison.

Words go unspoken, the strained silence so blaringly shrill and thick that it's hard to breathe or think. I know what I should do. What I should have done already. This girl has been spelled by our mortal enemy and that makes her my enemy. It's in my nature to hate her, to want to slaughter her. To crave the magic inside her so badly that it aches.

It aches, alright. Fuck, it aches.

"We're taught that magic has a price, and to save a life, you must take a life," she says, kicking down the walls we've built between us to shield our true selves. There's no hiding now. Truth has ripped us both wide open, exposing the scary, grotesque parts of our pasts that no one else wants to see.

"That's true," I manage to croak. Why am I telling her this? Why am I even entertaining this conversation?

"I know. Because my mother died a week later."

My eyes focus on the anguish etched underneath her perfectly guarded mask. "What?"

"Her family knew what had happened to me. They didn't approve of an … outsider meddling in our affairs. I believe they murdered her. I know what your kind thinks of us. I know that you see Voodoo as unnatural and a crime against nature."

"That's because it is. True magic comes only from the one real power, the Divine. Your gods are nothing more than false prophets. Frauds. That is why your mother died. A life for a life. The balance had to be restored."

She nods, those topaz eyes shining with crystalline tears. "So now you know how I know you. Why I hate you. My mother traded her life just so I could live long enough to meet my own death at the hands of pure, unrelenting evil. How's that for a trade off?" she laughs sardonically. "Growing up piss poor with a drunk for a father that never got over his wife's death. He looked at me with accusation everyday, knowing that it should have been me. All so I could one day be captured and forced into prostitution."

I don't correct her. I don't tell her that I won't force her into anything, and that her virtue is safe with me. I don't say that her hatred is misplaced, that I am just as confused about the meaning of her dreams and by her significance in my life. And I don't tell her that I won't kill her. That maybe the legends of the Dark being the first true evil are false, and that maybe I am more than just a soulless monster.

No. I don't say any of those things. I don't want to lie.

FIVE

"Get up."

I watch her as she blinks to consciousness, awareness settling into the tiny frown lines on her forehead. She sits up and stretches, then visibly flinches when she notices me sitting just feet away. "Holy shit, when'd you get here? What time is it?"

"Almost noon. Thought you might be hungry."

Amelie looks at the tray of covered dishes I've placed on the bed, and for the first time since I laid eyes on her, she almost … smiles. The aroma of tomato, onion and saffron waft from the heated plates and her stomach grumbles, causing her cheeks to blush scarlet.

"Looks like I was right," I chuckle, uncovering the dishes. I hand one to her and she digs in, barely pausing to breathe. She looks up at me with a mouthful when she feels my eyes on her.

"Sorry," she mumbles around rice and seafood.

I shake my head. "No, I should be apologizing. You've been a guest here, and I have been a less than gracious host. I should have fed you. Forgive me."

She stops mid chew, exposing the half eaten mush in her mouth. "You're shitting me, right? A guest? I was brought here under the intention of becoming a prostitute! This is hardly the Ramada."

"Yeah. About that … I have a proposition."

Amelie dabs her mouth with a napkin before narrowing her eyes at me. "A proposition? Like what? I'm not into any kinky bondage shit, you know. I mean, I'm not into anything, really."

I nod, stifling a grin at her choice of words. Kinky bondage shit? Yes, please. "I know. And I don't intend to force you, either. You will help out with some of the more domestic needs around here. The cooking, laundry…like a housekeeper of sorts. And when the debt has been fulfilled, you'll be free to go."

She raises a brow, the sour taste of skepticism puckering her full lips. "Free to go? Just like that?" Scraping the remnants of food on her plate, she shakes her head. "So what's in it for you? I'm not stupid. Your kind doesn't seem like the type to show mercy."

"I have questions that need answers. I believe that you are unaware that you were purposely sent, but this is no coincidence. I need to know why that is. If you are compliant, I will set you free."

"Ok," she shrugs. "Ask away. What do you want to know?"

I take a bite from my own plate, watching her as she assesses the movement of my mouth. She licks her own lips and a familiar heat floods my groin, causing my pants to go snug. Maybe I was wrong about her. Maybe she wants this. Wants *me*. Maybe, just maybe…

Her stomach growls, and my ego takes another blow. Awesome.

Without even acknowledging my wounded pride, I push the plate towards her, and am met with a small, appreciative, yet embarrassed smile. I'll take it.

"You sure?" she asks, already picking up the fork.

I nod once. "Sure. I'm not hungry anyway." Not for food, at least.

Amelie shovels a helping into her mouth, closing her eyes to savor the fusion of exotic, Spanish flavors. With anyone else, I'd be thoroughly repulsed, ready to shove their ill-mannered ass out of my sight. But with her, all I feel is … guilt? Or sympathy? Is that what I'm feeling?

No. Hell no.

"So," I begin, forcing myself to bury the unnamed emotion caught on the tip of my tongue. "Does anyone else know what you are? About your lineage?"

She shakes her head. "No. No one. I was taught to never tell anyone - that it could be dangerous."

"Yes, it is. You mustn't disclose that information. Understand?"

She nods, chewing slowly. I launch into my next question.

"When you got sick, how old were you?"

Grabbing a bottled water from the tray, she takes a swig before answering. "I was eight."

"So that would make you…"

"Eighteen. The day your men came for my father - the day they brought me here - was my birthday."

I mentally summarize the last forty eight hours. Hard to believe that, in the span of two days, my life has been completely tipped off its axis by this mysterious, captivating, utterly infuriating creature. Seems like so long ago. The women I've had in this very bed have been long forgotten, their lives only a mere whisper of a memory. When you've lived as long as I have, fucked and killed through nearly two centuries, it all becomes a blur. Faces begin to blend together. Even sex feels the same - almost choreographed. I've done it all, I've seen it all. Nothing surprises me.

Except Amelie.

Her scent, her soul, those uncanny eyes tainted with Light magic … it's a dangerous concoction that draws me to her, pulling me deeper into the unknown. Maybe it's the thrill of chasing death. Of diving into my inevitable demise and ending the monotony of this life. Because when you have it all, there's nothing else to live for. Nothing to strive to achieve. Your story has already been told, over and over again.

"That was your birthday?" I can't even hide the scowl painted on my face. Fuck it.

"Yeah," she shrugs. "But it's ok. Not like my father remembered or anything."

I shake my head in disgust. "The Light have a thing for significant dates. Pretentious assholes," I mutter. "My apologies."

Amelie frowns, and I feel the sudden urge to wrap her in my arms and kiss the little lines in her forehead. "For what?"

"I don't know," I shrug. "Your father. The Light imposing on your eighteenth birthday. Me being a fucking prick and not feeding you. Take your pick."

"Not all of those things were your fault." She fingers a wayward dark brown curl. "I'm sorry, too. For saying those things about you. You obviously had no idea that I was cursed. And honestly … not everything I saw in those dreams was bad."

My eyebrows reach for the crown of my head, and I swear, my voice goes up an octave. "Oh?"

"Yeah. I mean, the sex and stuff was pretty gross, especially when I was a kid, but sometimes you seemed…nice. Normal. And a little bit lonely."

I bite back a snort of protest. Me? Lonely? How the hell can you be lonely when you're constantly surrounded by people that need you? Want you? Crave to be near you just for a tiny slice of the royal pie? I roll my eyes and give her a playful smirk.

"Except … except when you were with this one guy," Amelie continues. "He cared for you, looked after you. You always seemed happy when he was around. Maybe even a bit relieved, if that makes sense. He looks like you, a little older. Like maybe a brother or cousin. And he's, uh, really, *really* good looking."

That empty, hollow ache returns, attacking my chest with the frigid chill of remembrance. Amelie may have shared my memories, but she will never understand the pain of abandonment that haunted me for decades after Dorian left. He could have taken me with him - shit, I practically fucking begged him to - but he was too far-gone to even think about what he was leaving me with. The weight of our father's expectations now rested solely on my shoulders. He was determined to create the perfect heir with or without my brother. And he wouldn't stop until he accomplished just that … or until I broke.

A soft, delicate hand grazes my arm, kindling the surface of my skin, before swiftly pulling away. Amelie looks at me with an embarrassed gleam in her eyes. "Who is he?" she whispers.

"My brother." The words are out of my mouth before I think to stop them. "Dorian. But he's gone now."

"I'm sorry," she replies, regret painting her face. "When did he die?"

I shrug and shake my head simultaneously, unable to come up with a logical explanation. "I don't know. I don't even know if he is dead. I just know that a long time ago, he left and never looked back."

"And you miss him." It's not a question. The answer is already written on my face.

"Everyday."

"You'll see him again," Amelie states with certainty as if she knows the first thing about me or my family, or the curse of being birthed into this life. I want to tell her that she's wrong, that she's no more than a stupid girl who doesn't know a goddamn thing about the Dark. But the hope that shines so bright in those peculiar eyes keeps me from refuting her blind faith. It's what keeps me hanging onto that beautiful lie, in hopes that her ignorance will not be in vain.

Her dreams brought her to me. Maybe they'll bring Dorian back home. Hell, maybe they'll even give purpose to the shallow carcass of a man that is me. Either way, this girl was sent for a reason - sent to *me* for a reason. I just don't know if it's to kill her or fuck her. Hurt her or heal her. Hate her or lo…

Never mind.

"Here's what I'm thinking," I blurt out, quickly changing course, tugging at the long layers of my hair in frustration. "I don't think your illness was spontaneous. It seems very meditated … deliberate."

Amelie frowns. "What? You think someone purposely made me sick?"

"Definitely. It wasn't random. Choosing you - the descendant of Marie Laveau - was no accident. They knew what they were doing."

Amelie fondles the bottle cap of her water, chewing her cherry red lips in deliberation. "And by *they* you mean the Light, right? But that doesn't make sense. Aren't they known for healing and goodness? And why sicken an innocent child just to heal her?"

I stifle the sardonic chuckle building in my chest. "Isn't it obvious? So you'd be in their debt. The Light aren't the righteous fuckers they'd like everyone to believe they are. They're no different from the Dark. We're just more honest."

"I don't believe that," she says shaking her head. But the doubt is already written on her face. She knows there is some truth to my explanation.

"Tell me, pretty girl, what do your Voodoo ancestors believe they know about the Light? What is their theory on your mysterious illness?"

"They believe I was cursed," she shrugs, rolling her eyes. "My mother refused to fully accept what they stood for and my sickness was the result of her betrayal. All bullshit if you ask me. Marie Laveau was known as a saint. Why would someone that stood for good be ok with hurting a child? They worshipped her memory, yet they had strayed so far beyond her teachings that she's probably rolling in her grave."

I raise a cocky brow and lean forward. "You do know that's a crock of shit, right?"

"What?"

"Oh dear, sweet, naive Amelie." I realize it's the first time I've uttered her name aloud, and the impulse to do it again is undeniable. I can't fight it- I don't want to. It's stronger than me, penetrating skin and bone and guiding my tongue like a marionette. *"Amelie."*

"Oui, Oui, Monsieur Nikolai," she jibes in perfect French, a ghost of a smile on her lips. Suddenly, I can't even remember what I was saying. All I can see, all I can even focus on are those lips. How they curve as they wrap around my name. How they feel, how they taste. How badly I want to feel them against my skin, burning straight to my soul.

"Did you dream about me? Before I woke you?" My voice is low and raspy, and I can't help but move in closer to her. My eyes tingle with cold, but every other part of my body is warm with expectation.

"Yes," she utters, her own voice a mere husky whisper.

I move closer still. "And what did you see?"

Amelie chews her lip, those magnificent eyes lowered in apprehension. She looks so innocent. Girlish and pure.

"You, here in this room, in this bed … with me."

Six

"You've got to be kidding me," Amelie says, holding up the black and white frilly frock. "I'm not wearing this."

I recline on the king sized bed, trying not to laugh as Amelie assesses the French Maid outfit. It's mid morning, three days after she was brought to me. Three days after my very existence was altered.

Yesterday, we spent almost the entire day talking. She told me about the life she left behind, her family, her friends. I gave her vague explanations of Light and Dark magic as she listened intently, her eyes bright with curiosity. She didn't seem afraid, nor even one bit repulsed. Even as I explained how we survive, she simply nodded, taking it all in. It was … odd. Different. And exhilarating. I had never spoken to another human for more than a few moments, and usually only to command them to do what I wanted. *Get on your knees and suck. Bend over. Spread your legs.*

I had never had that with … anyone, I realized. I only consorted with my own kind so I didn't have the need to explain shit to them. And I wouldn't dream of even hinting at my true nature to a human. But Amelie was different. I felt at ease with her. Hell, I felt safe with her, yet I knew I could destroy her without even trying. And in the back of my mind, buried under denial and secrets, I knew that was still a real possibility.

I watch as Amelie turns the racy garb from front to back, searching for the rest of the fabric, and I can't help but chuckle. "Standard uniform, sweetheart."

Her eyes grow wide with disbelief. "Are you serious? Why? Who in their right mind would think this is appropriate to wash clothes and mop the floor in?"

I look around the room with raised brows. "Um, you do remember where you are, right? This is a place of fantasy and illusions. A depraved charade. Everyone has a part to play, and we always stay in character."

"Bu-but … this is just so … wrong," she pouts.

"Hey, the other girls wear much less. Shall I grab one of their getups for you?"

"No! No, that won't be necessary," she huffs. "And I suppose the high heeled Mary Janes are all part of the fantasy too."

"Obviously," I reply, running a hand through my hair. Amelie tips her head to one side and appraises the movement through narrowed eyes.

"You'd look better if you cut your hair."

"Excuse me?" I ask in mock offense.

"I mean, you, uh, I … never mind. Forget I said anything." She goes back to fiddling with the costume in her hands, yet her rosy cheeks tell me that she's far from over the comment.

"No. I want to hear it." Without thinking, I gently graze her chin, guiding her head up to meet my gaze. The burn is there, yet it pales in comparison to the other parts of me that are on fire. "Tell me, please."

She shrugs but makes no move to remove herself from my touch. Instead, she takes it a step further, and reaches her hand up to my head to softly run her fingers through my hair. "It's just, you have great hair and all, but it's always in your face. And it ages you. You should trim it a bit or brush it back. Let people *see* you."

See me? Why the hell would I ever want that?

"I'm not so sure people would like what they see," I reply quietly, instantly regretting it. It's too personal, too … honest.

A genuine smile graces her lips, making those ethereal eyes sparkle against the backdrop of her dark, lush waves. "I find that hard to believe, Nikolai."

"Well, maybe you're just gullible," I reply, feeling the corners of my own mouth pull into a sincere grin. "And I told you yesterday

- call me Niko."

Dropping her hand, she bashfully shrugs away from my touch, and I instantly feel the coldness return. Damp, dark emptiness. In the span of a few short days, Amelie has become as warm and bright as the sun to me. She's become my light, and I never thought in a million years, in an eternity of existing in the dark, that I could ever crave that.

I know this feeling isn't real - it can't be. It's a trick, a lie. Even still, I want it. I want to step into the sun with her. I want her smile to warm me from the inside out. I want those bright eyes to pierce into my soul and see ... more ... in me. I've barely touched this girl, yet she knows more about me than anyone in this entire world. She's has ten years of memories - my memories - to prove it. And, in that fact, I find comfort.

"Niko, huh? Are there a lot of Nikos in Greece?" she asks folding her tan, bare legs on the bed. The edges of her tiny, silk sleep shorts ride up her thigh a bit, and I silently thank Nadia for providing such fascinating sleepwear. I'll have to give her a raise.

"There are, but none quite like me," I reply, forcing myself to divert my appreciative eyes. What the fuck? Me practicing restraint? Talk about turning over a new leaf. Uprooting a giant oak is more like it.

"I'd say," Amelie blushes. "So ... will I be moving into one of the other rooms now that I officially have a job here?"

I train my face to wear the same passive, easygoing expression, though inside I'm a fucking mosh pit of misplaced fury. I don't want her to leave my room. Fuck, there's no way I can breathe without knowing she is here, safe with me. The past few days have been some of the most enlightening, meaningful days of my life. And while we haven't done much more than talk and sleep side by side – well, she'd sleep and I'd watch like some pathetic, pimply-faced kid that jerks off to his mom's lingerie catalogs - I couldn't imagine not having her in my bed. I've never felt such peace, such ... happiness. Knowing that she was just inches way, dreaming of *me*. I'd drive myself crazy with the possibilities. What did she see when she closed those mesmerizing eyes? Did it make her want me, just as badly as I want her?

Realizing that she's waiting for an answer, I give a sly half smile and shrug. "Well … the rooms here are for the working girls, if you know what I mean. I have to make sure that there is available space here for them and their … guests. Now, if you'd like to rethink your job title, I'd be happy to arrange that and get you moved in immediately."

Amelie's eyes go wide, and she shakes her head furiously. "Oh, no. Absolutely not. I'd much rather stay here. You know … if it's ok with you." She bites her lip and looks away. "I can understand if you want me to go. I'm sure I'm seriously cramping your style. We can work out a system, you know. Maybe leave a sock on the door if you have company, or I can stay with someone else. I don't particularly like having a live porno played out in front of me." She turns to me and smiles, though it doesn't touch her eyes. "Ten years of seeing every inch of you and more women than I can count … no wonder I've never had a boyfriend."

"Wait a minute … you've never had a boyfriend?" I frown, choosing to focus on that part of her oration.

"Kinda hard, ya know. Piss poor, drunk father, crazy Voodoo family, inexplicable nightly dreams of a murderous, philandering Warlock ... Oh yeah, guys were lining up around the block."

I know she's joking, but a pang of guilt attacks my chest. How much of this girl's misfortune have I been responsible for? Her father has gambled and drank in casinos and bars that I own. She was cursed with a mysterious illness, so the Light could sink their claws into her to get to me. She's been plagued with nightmares of my evil doings for a decade, no doubt warding off any hopes of intimacy. And the biggest bearer of my guilt? The tense, violent history between the Laveaus and the Dark - something I played a part in.

This is it. The opportunity for me to prove that I'm more than some pretentious asshole and own what the fuck I am for once. The chance for me to put bullshit and ancient family secrets aside and do what's right for me. To do what's in my heart, no matter how black and vacant it is.

"Amelie," I begin, my voice shakier than it's ever been, the authoritative timbre gone. "There's something you should know…"

She tilts her head to one side, and gives me a small, sweet smile of encouragement.

I open my mouth to speak my truth, to confess my sins, to bare my soul and pray for understanding. But before the words can escape, the sound of approaching footsteps puts me on guard, and the shame and humility is replaced with hostility and possessiveness.

Three raps reverberate the door seconds later. Against my better judgment, I call out, "Enter."

Varshaun opens the door, dressed in his usual black three-piece suit. His dark hair is pulled back into a ponytail, and his bronze skin looks even darker paired with his aqua eyes. He has scented her, and the hungry gleam in those eyes shine with craving.

"What is it?" I snap, agitated by his mere presence. Varshaun frowns but quickly replaces it with a mischievous grin. His teeth look more like razor sharp fangs, and a sudden impulse inside me tempts me to knock that smile right off his face.

I shake the insane thoughts from my muddled head. What the hell is wrong with me? This is my best friend - someone who has been my brother for over a century. Being in Amelie's proximity is seriously fucking with my rationale. The only logical explanation has to be the mix of Light magic in her Voodoo blood.

Varshaun steps farther into the room, and his eyes roam from my angry expression to Amelie, and then back to me. "I see the two of you are getting along splendidly." His gaze drifts to Amelie's smooth, bare legs and up to her supple breasts before landing on her full, red lips. Feeling the intrusion of his lustful glare, she brings her knees up to her chest and hugs her legs, shielding her precious, delicate body. "I knew you'd like this one, Niko. She's special, isn't she? Bet she's quite the amusing ride."

Before he can say another word, in a blur of frustration, confusion and distrust, without even bothering to hide my abilities from Amelie, I am in front of him, my blue eyes growing colder and paler by the second. "What brings you to my quarters, old friend?" I ask through clenched teeth.

Varshaun narrows his eyes at my offensive stance and smirks. "Well, seeing as I am your friend and business manager, I was concerned to learn that you've been too...." He looks over my shoulder, glimpsing Amelie's frightened frame on the bed. "...preoccupied to handle some of the professional matters. I thought surely that you were ill." A devilish half grin crawls onto his lips. He's baiting me. He knows it's impossible for us to get sick.

"I'm fine, as you can see. And what professional matters do you speak of? That's what I pay you for, correct?"

"You're right," Varshaun nods. "Forgive my intrusion. But I must say, Niko, I'm wounded. What happened to my boy? One little human girl has caused you to abandon me and leave me to slay the women of New Orleans alone? Surely, that is not the case."

Varshaun, you cunning, meddlesome sonofabitch.

I huff out an irritated breath before turning to face Amelie. "I'll leave you to get ready. Nadia has you in the kitchen today. Report there when you're finished and they'll give you instruction."

"Ok," she whispers through trembling lips.

I nod, before turning away from her sad eyes. Varshaun opens the door, a satisfied grin on his face.

"Niko?" Amelie calls quietly before I can cross the threshold. I turn to her more eagerly than I should.

"Yes?"

"After I'm done today, later tonight ... should I find somewhere else to stay? I hate to bother you and you never answered my question earlier, but if you want me to, I can..."

"No," I reply before she can get out the words. "No. Stay. I want you to stay... here. With me. Ok?" I hold my breath, awaiting her reaction and dreading the onslaught of questions from Varshaun.

"Ok," she finally nods. "I'll be here."

"You wanna explain what the fuck I just witnessed?"

I continue to walk down Bourbon Street, looking straight ahead. I was able to elude Varshaun's shocked glare burning a hole in the side of my head while we were back at the house amongst dozens of listening ears, but now that we're alone, there's no way he's letting me off the hook.

"What's there to explain?" I reply flatly.

"Um, excuse me, but how about starting with the hot brunette you've got stashed in your room? I mean, I get it. Maybe she's too good to share … I've been there. But you want her to stay with you? Like actually sleep in your room? For more than a night?"

I look at my most trusted friend and nearly flinch at the look of sheer puzzlement on his face. He's right. Now that someone's said it aloud, it does sound ludicrous.

"It's only temporary. She has … something I need. And I need her close in order to get it."

"Ah," Varshaun nods. "You've gotten yourself a taste of some Grade A pussy. So good and sweet that you crave it all the time. Need a fix like a fiend. Congrats, my friend." He claps me on the back and moves in closer to my ear. "Let me know when you're finished with her. I'd like to sample that luscious creature. Even better, we could fuck her together, like old times. A little double penetration will help rid that shyness."

I clench my fists so hard that my bones crack. I can feel my nails breaking the skin of my palms, causing fresh, warm blood to pool in my hands. I want to hurt him. Fuck, I want to kill him. I want to rip his fucking pretty boy head off and tie it to the nearest flagpole by those long, black locks. But instead, I plaster on a tight grin, trying desperately to appear normal. And normal for me is ten times worse than Varshaun.

"No," I say shaking my head stiffly. "She's not ready for that. I have special plans for that girl." And none of them involve double penetration, Varshaun, or any other motherfucker for that matter.

"Suit yourself," he shrugs. "Just don't kill her before I get a taste."

My pisstivity takes a backseat to bewilderment, and I raise a brow in question.

"Oh yeah, I know about the two girls from the other night. You sure you're ok, man? You've been edgy. I mean, accidents happen, but you haven't drained someone in years, let alone two girls at once."

I shake my head, unable to verbally explain myself. I know what has caused my ire.

Amelie.

As badly as I want her for … I don't even know what, her mere presence has me off my game. I desire her body, but I crave her soul. I admire her mind, but I need her heart. I'm seriously a clusterfuck of emotion, and no magic in the world can undo the spell she has me under.

I can't even express this shit to my closest friend. The only person I can talk to is Amelie. She's the only one who'd understand, the only person that has truly glimpsed my soul, and the very person that can never know how I feel.

I look around, realizing that we've wandered into a part of the French Quarter that we don't usually frequent. It's an area that we've somewhat deemed enemy territory. "Why are we here?"

Varshaun hops up the steps of the ornate mansion, mischief etched on his face. "Just paying our friend Malcolm a little visit. Heard he was having a hard time keeping his girls on a short leash."

I follow him up the steps but pause at the top, shaking my head. "Malcolm is insignificant and so are his girls. There's enough money in this city for everyone. Let him be. If we catch it, we'll deal with it."

The irises of Varshaun's eyes turn dark and tumultuous. "There are rules, my friend. Rules put in place by your family at that. You can't let them think you're weak. If you let this slide, you're just opening the door for others to defy you. And we wouldn't want Daddy Dearest to get wind of that."

Dammit, he's right.

I take a deep breath and follow Varshaun to the front door. It's early, so none of his girls are out displaying their goods on the balcony and porch. Funny how the dark and depraved thrive at night, as if the shadows can conceal our iniquities. Under the dark cloak of denial, we feed our inner beasts with our own individual brands of evil, stifling the guilt until morning. Avoidance is a way of life for us sinners. Maybe we aren't so honest after all.

Without even bothering to knock, Varshaun turns the doorknob. When it doesn't click open, he steps back, turning to give me an impish grin. His eyes spark with white flames, and with a simple exhale, he blows the front door wide open. The heavy wood frame shakes and groans as if it had been propelled with hurricane force winds. As graceful and fluid as ever, Varshaun steps inside, not rattled in the least.

"I told you, little pigs, what happens when you don't let me in," he calls out to an audience of stunned, terrified faces. Prostitutes, both women and men, scurry out of the way, shielding their half naked bodies. "I'll huff, and I'll puff, and I'll blow your house down."

I roll my eyes, and step into the vast home, not at all impressed with Varshaun's theatrics. Normally, his zest for drama would have provoked a little shameless fun, but today, my head … my heart … is just not into it.

"What in the hell is going on out here?" a squatty, bald man spits, waddling his way from a back room wearing nothing but a silk bathrobe. His beady eyes find us standing in the middle of the great room. A ring of frightened bystanders looks to him for guidance.

"Mr. V? Mr. N? What are you doing here? Forgive me. I wasn't aware you'd be dropping by."

Varshaun holds up a palm, halting further explanation. "Oh, don't look so surprised, Malcolm. Surely you knew we'd be interested in all paranormal activity performed outside of regulation. Tell me, have your whores finally managed to fuck your brains out? Or are you really that stupid?"

Malcolm reluctantly stumbles towards us, trembling and sweating like a filthy pig. "Mr. V, I can assure you that my girls had nothing to do with whatever transgression you are talking about. They've broken no laws, I can attest to that."

"Is that right, Malcolm? So none of your girls turned any tricks outside of your district? And none of them were responsible for fooling three of *my* kind into breathing them, only to manipulate their minds?"

Fucking necromancers. They're Voodoo witches that dabble in strong black magic with the ability to control supernatural creatures. Legend tells us that a necromancer with enough power has the ability to completely overtake the mind and actions of a Dark One. With that kind of magic at their disposal, they could demolish entire cities.

Of course, none of us have actually witnessed it in action. Every so often, we'll stumble upon a Warlock that has experienced holes in his memory. Usually, it's from a soul-sucker, or a fiend. Yes, even the Dark has addicts. They get addicted to the power and have to constantly replenish in order maintain their strength. Soon, the craving becomes too strong, and just a taste of magic won't do. They seek out human witches for their fix, opening themselves to become susceptible to their Voodoo poison.

I tune out Malcolm's blubbering as he tries to refute Varshaun's claims and take a look around. Audible gasps ring out as my gaze shifts to a group huddled on the couch. They're terrified of us, trembling in a haze of horrified confusion. They've heard the stories, maybe even seen one of us in action. But me … I'm an anomaly. In public, Varshaun is the mouthpiece. I rarely ever accompany him in situations like these. A Dark prince wreaking havoc on the streets of New Orleans would put our entire family at risk. So, I keep quiet and give Varshaun the spotlight, feeding his never-ending ego.

Still, everyone knows I'm not to be fucked with. Call it instinct or a sixth sense, they can feel the way the tiny hairs on their arms stand upright whenever I'm near. They notice the drop in the temperature, the sudden density in the air. That niggling voice in the back of their heads that tell them to run and not look back. I am the supreme evil, a force so dark and dangerous that even grown men quake in my presence.

The whimpers grow louder as I take a step towards the group of bystanders, and something in my little black heart rejoices. Ah, yes. Fear. Like fucking candy to the Dark. The taste for it developing on my tongue, my mouth curls into a devilish smirk before I wink an icy blue eye, causing the light bulbs in the room to pop and shatter. Shrieks ring out, and I bark out a hearty laugh. What's the point in having all this power if you can't have a little fun?

I approach a young woman quivering on the carpet. Her gaze instantly drops to the floor and I crouch before her to meet her eyes.

"Look at me, little one," I command. Reluctantly, she lifts her head, giving me access to her big brown eyes. She's beautiful, her skin smooth as silk, the color of sweet chocolate. "That's right. Good girl."

Her curly tendrils frame her face in a wild, exotic style and I reach out to gently stroke the dark coils. She instantly relaxes, her wide eyes still locked onto mine. "Now that you're calm, I have a few questions for you, pretty girl. Do you know who I am?"

"No, sir," she squeaks, her voice light and high pitched, with a thick Yat accent.

"Good," I smile. "Do you know *what* I am?"

"No, sir."

"Good. That's very good. Do you work here, sweetheart?"

"Yes, sir," she answers without hesitance. Feeling the pull of my influence mixed with her carnal desire, she moves into my touch. Her dark eyes grow hot and sultry, and her nipples pucker under her thin satin slip.

"And how old are you?"

The girl captures my hand in her own and brings it to her lips, kissing the palm. "Fifteen, but Malcolm makes me tell people I'm nineteen." When I frown and pull my hand free, she scrambles forward, nearly climbing onto my lap. "But I swear I'm good! I'm one of the best here. Malcolm even says I'm his favorite. He said my young, tight pussy feels like heaven and tastes as sweet as a hot fudge sundae. And that I give the best head in three parishes."

Bile rises in my throat, and my irises tingle with fury. "No need, dear one. No need to worry about that ever again."

I'm on my feet in a blur of blistering rage and cross the room just as Varshaun finishes his tirade.

"The next time I even suspect any of your girls stepping out of bounds, I'll do more than blow open the fucking door," he warns him. "Do you understand?"

"Y-yes, Mr. V. If I find any of my girls have broken the rules, I'll kill them myself," he stammers, beads of sweat rolling down his fat face. He exhales a sigh of relief when Varshaun nods and turns to retreat. Little does he know, V is the least of his problems.

"Listen to me, you fat fuck," I hiss, moving in so close that I smell the vile odor of his rapid breaths. "You're done using underage girls. So done, that you will return them to their homes plus compensate them all for exploiting them. Let's say twenty grand each, plus you'll ensure they get into decent schools. Doesn't that sound fair?"

"Wha-? Twenty grand? I don't have that kind of money!" he screeches indignantly, causing revolting spittle to fly from his mouth.

"You heard me, you sick fucker. Twenty grand. And if you don't have the cash, I suggest you find a good realtor. You have three days."

I spin on my heel and make my way to the door where Varshaun waits, wearing a delighted grin. My eyes spot the young girl with the spiral curls, and I nod to her. Her big, brown eyes shine with grateful tears.

"It's not like they didn't want it, you know," Malcolm calls out from behind my back, obviously delirious. I pause mid-step, my trembling fists tight at my sides. "They begged for it. Pussy is pussy, no matter how old it is. As long as it can grow a bush, it's fuckable."

My mind instantly goes to Amelie. She could've been one of these girls. She could've been the girl with the curly, brown hair, used and abused at such a tender age. What if it was Malcolm that her father was indebted to? What if she was forced to offer her body to him in exchange for her father's life?

"You know, on second thought…" I turn around to face his deranged scowl, blind rage clouding my rationale. "I really, *really* hate child molesters."

I raise my palm, spreading my fingers as they become engulfed in blue fire. Simultaneously, Malcolm's limbs go rigid and his mouth falls slack, completely immobilized. His muddy brown eyes are filled with terror as he tries to struggle against the invisible restraints. Drool drips from the corner of his disgusting mouth.

"Shhhh," I say in his ear. "Don't fight it. It will all be over soon, you piece of shit. You won't be able to abuse another child again. Now … along with child molesters, I despise spineless men. And you, dear Malcolm, are spineless."

Malcolm grunts out a tearful response as I circle his grotesque frame. Dozens watch with rapt attention, yet none of them step up to save their employer. They have no love, no loyalty for him.

"Yes, yes, I agree," I nod, responding to his indecipherable groans. I stop in front of him and smooth the silken fabric on his meaty shoulders. "You really aren't completely spineless. But that can definitely be arranged."

With my hand still covered in blue flames, I sink it into Malcolm's gut, spearing through blubber, tissue and vital organs.

Screams ring out all over the mansion, masking his muffled cries of pain. Yes, pain. Though he may not be able to move, he can feel everything. He can feel me clawing my way through his flesh with razor-sharp talons. Can feel the blood gushing from the gaping hole in his abdomen. And when my hand wraps around his spine, he can feel every-fucking-thing as I rip it from his body.

"There you go, motherfucker," I say, dropping the blood-slick bones to the floor just as Malcolm takes his last pathetic breath. I release the hold on his body and it crumples to the floor in a bloody heap. "Now, you're really spineless."

I look around at the array of panicked faces staring back at me. "You all are free to go," I call out, loud enough for my voice to echo throughout the grand house. "However, if you wish to stay, you can be sure that you'll be provided with sufficient living conditions, pay and healthcare, as well as protection. And if you are younger than the age of eighteen, a car will be sent this afternoon to take you home to your families."

As if on cue, the young girl approaches me, holding out a towel. Graciously, I take it, wiping away Malcolm's putrid blood and guts that extend all the way up to my elbow. Fuck. Another suit ruined. But as I look down at the young girl, and the other grateful faces surrounding me, I know that I've done the right thing. I've chosen to be *better*.

SEVEN

I lay on my back on top of the satin, ornate comforter, my head resting on top of my hands … and I smile.

Amelie is showering in the en suite bathroom just feet away, and images of her naked and wet, with only tiny suds kissing her most intimate places, are engrained in my head, causing my cock to ache with need.

It's been nearly two weeks since I had sex. Two weeks of sleeping chastely next to Amelie's tight, delicious body. Two weeks of feeling the warmth of her smile. Two weeks of letting someone see me for the very first time, and not being afraid of the rejection. Laughing heartily at her corny jokes. Listening intently as she tells me stories of her old neighborhood and growing up on the wrong side of the tracks. Teaching her how to play chess, and in turn, her teaching me how to play Gin Rummy. Watching her delicate eyelids flutter as vivid dreams of me visit her subconscious.

I smile.

Because for the first time in nearly two centuries, I have found happiness.

I thought it was that feeling I got whenever business was spectacularly good. Or the sensation I felt during amazing sex. I even thought I had achieved it when my father agreed to let me run all Gulf Coast operations, allowing me to prove to him and myself that I was more than a spoiled royal brat.

I was wrong. Amelie is my happiness. Being with her, knowing her, letting her know me, is the epitome of bliss.

"What's with the crazy eyes and serial killer smile?" a sweet, playful voice asks. "You plottin' on me?"

I look over just as Amelie crosses the room towards the bed, wearing nothing but a navy silk sleep shirt that stops right at the middle of her shapely thighs. I do everything in my power to force my eyes up to her face. Holy fuck. Is she trying to kill me?

"Well, if I told you, I'd have to kill you," I jibe, hoping to mask the longing in my voice.

Amelie kneels on the bed, drying her damp hair with a towel. "Hmmm, those are mighty big words for a pretty boy prince," she retorts. "Don't forget - I'm from Ninth Ward, buddy. I can and will kick your ass."

We both break into guffaws at her ridiculous comment. I sit up, bringing our bodies closer together, and stilling all laughter. Our gazes collide for long, silent seconds before Amelie looks away, a scarlet blush painting her cheeks.

"Don't you find this kinda ... weird?" she asks quietly.

"What's weird?"

"I don't know," she answers with a shrug. "One day, you're ready to murder me and I'm hating you, and the next it's ... different. Like it's easy and casual and fun, and I actually find myself looking at you as a decent guy, and not some monster. Because to me, now that I know you, you're not. You're nothing like I expected."

"Well, what did you expect?" I ask, tipping my head to one side.

"Crazed, soul-sucking lunatic that just goes around screwing anything on two legs and killing without a second thought?"

A few weeks ago that assessment would have probably been spot on. I don't have the heart to tell her.

"Sorry to disappoint you, sweetheart."

"Oh, I'm not disappointed," she says, shaking her head. "I'm relieved. Be kind of a buzz-kill to be sleeping next to some demented murderer. Talk about awkward."

I flinch and my mouth pulls down into a grimace before I can stop myself. Those amber irises pick up on the switch in my expression immediately, and Amelie frowns. "Hey, what's wrong?"

"Nothing," I reply, with a stiff shake of my head. I can't meet her eyes. It's in those depths that I am the most vulnerable, the most honest.

"No, it's not *nothing.* Come on, Niko. You've asked me a million questions and I've answered them all truthfully. Now if I've said something to offend you, you have to tell me. I don't want you smothering me in my sleep or something because you're pissed at me." She offers a small smile, but I don't return it.

"I'm not going to hurt you, ok?" I snap. "I told you that. So just drop it."

Amelie reels back, confusion and hurt darkening her face. "Whoa. Ok, I'm sorry. I didn't mean that. It was a bad joke."

I shake my head again and look away, disgusted with what she must see in me at this very moment. She's right, and I don't deserve her. I don't even deserve to breathe the same air as her. If I can't be honest with myself, how the hell can I be honest with her? If I can't accept what I am, how can I expect that of her?

"I have to tell you something," I finally say, my head still turned.

"Ok," she replies with a quiet, strained voice.

I take a deep breath and release it, letting go of fear and reluctance. If I want Amelie to trust me with her heart, I have to be honest with her. I have to earn it. I have to be better than what I was before.

"The day that Varshaun came to get me, we had some business to tend to in the Quarter." I look back at her, my eyes gleaming with apology. "What was supposed to be a quick, routine stop turned ... dark."

"Ok," she says again, prompting me to go on.

"Have you ever heard of Malcolm Boisseau?"

A look of sheer disgust flashes across her face, answering my question. I don't even wait for her to tell me how she knows him. The answer may push me to the brink of violence.

"We followed up on a tip that Malcolm's girls were engaging in black magic, which is forbidden in this city. And while we were there, something literally fell into my lap." I run a hand through my hair and pull at the ends in frustration. "Amelie ... I found out he was not only exploiting young girls, he was having sex with them too. He was fucking molesting children."

Amelie gasps and claps a hand over her mouth in horror. "Oh my God," she says, letting it fall to her heart. "Oh my God, that's terrible! How did y-...Wait. What do you mean he *was?*"

I'm frozen in place, held by those penetrating eyes that seem to strip me bare to my soul. I don't know how to tell her; I can't find the words. I've killed dozens of times without shame, without an inkling of remorse or regret. I've done it for power, for revenge, hell, I've done it for fun. But now... now that my newfound conscience has taken the reins, I can't even find it in me to confess my sins, no matter how justified they are.

"Tell me, Niko... tell me what happened," Amelie says just above a whisper.

Tentatively, she reaches her hand towards me, her solemn gaze asking permission. I remain stock-still, holding my breath. Not because I have some weird phobia about touching - shit, physicality is all I know - but because it's her touching me, her comforting me. Her showing me just a smidgen of affection. And right now, as her delicate hand rests on top of mine before sliding to my palm to interlace our fingers, I feel like she's breaking me down, ripping me open. Taking every fucking defense I had and demolishing them with a sledgehammer. I'm the one helpless and weak spread out beneath her. I'm the one begging for her mercy, completely at her will.

Tiny golden sparks meld with blue, before dying into a simmer on our skin. It hurts. It's sweet agony and torturous bliss. It's everything I never knew I wanted.

"Amelie," a voice rasps from somewhere deep within me. "I killed him. I killed that sick sonofabitch. And I liked it. I loved it. And I'm sorry."

She doesn't speak. I don't even know if she's looking at me. All

I can see are our fingers intertwined, that small part of us holding onto…something. Something much bigger than the both of us.

"Thank you," she finally whispers.

My eyes dart to her face to find a soft smile on her lips, a look of admiration in her eyes. A look I've never been gifted with in all my years.

"For what?"

"For telling me. And for saving those girls. And for ensuring that he never hurts another child again."

"But…but now you know how vile I am. Now you know I'm a killer."

An unexpected chuckle bubbles from her chest. "Niko, I've always known you were a killer. Don't forget that I've borne witness to your antics for the last ten years. I'm not saying I'm ok with murder. I'm totally against it, actually. But what you did today wasn't murder, it was redemption. It was justice. It was necessary."

We fall asleep side by side, like always, but with our hands clasped together. Funny how such a chaste gesture can be so profound, so deeply intimate. I've never felt closer to another soul, not even when I was buried inside them, breathing their life into mine. And I now that I've felt it, I never want to let it go. I never want to let *her* go.

I feel Amelie jerk in the night, and her hand is squeezing mine with enough pressure to cut off circulation. My eyes snap open immediately and I am hovering over her, clutching her shoulders.

"No, no, no," she cries, large tears spilling down the sides of her face. Her closed eyelids flutter rapidly and she's covered with sweat. "No, please, no. Please come back to me. Don't leave me!"

"Amelie," I call out, shaking her gently. "Amelie, wake up. You're having a nightmare."

"Oh God, no! Please! I'll do anything…no, no, no!" Her body

trembles uncontrollably, piquing my alarm. I have to do something. I have to help her.

"Amelie! Amelie, listen to me. Wake up!" Panic growing in my chest, I sweep a hand over her forehead, a single finger doused in blue flames.

Nothing.

Fuck.

Her body convulses even more, and I know this is more than a simple dream. I shake her harder, both hands now ignited. "Come on, Amelie! Wake up! Fucking wake up now!"

Her body goes still and her whimpers cease. I don't even think she's breathing, though I can clearly hear the pounding of her heart. I hold onto that sliver of hope. She's still with me.

Just as my hand caresses her damp cheek, Amelie's eyes snap open, her retinas as black as onyx. This isn't magic. It's not even natural. It's evil.

Before I can even think to react, she trains her black, sinister glare on me as she grabs my hand, squeezing it until I can feel my bones crack.

"You will pay, demon. You will pay in blood," a bone chilling voice spits. It's not even remotely close to her harmonious tone. "They're coming, and you will pay! You will burn for what you have done. Burn, demon!"

I yank my hand away from her tight grasp just as her eyes shut and her body sags in unnatural slumber. My whole body shakes, ice cold tingles running through my pulsing veins. My instincts tell me to kill her now. To reach into her chest and pulverize her heart with my bare hands. Whatever she's possessed with needs a beating heart, and I won't let it take her. I won't let it take my Amelie.

With a shaky hand, I reach toward her, just barely touching the space where her most precious, vital organ lay protected. I don't want to, but I don't know what else to do. I don't have any other choice.

Her hand suddenly grasps mine, but this time, the touch is soft, gentle. She pulls it closer to her, clutching it to her heart. Once again, her eyes open wide … and bright. Golden irises look back at me, filling the room with brilliant, blinding light.

"Help her," a voice whispers. It isn't her voice, but it's trill and feminine, not a hint of malice. "Save her."

"How?" I find myself asking with trembling lips. I don't even know who - or what - I'm talking to, but nothing else matters other than saving Amelie's life.

"To save her, you must know love," the small voice says. "You must love her."

Then all is black. Still.

Dark.

The room is silent and cold with only the rhythm of Amelie's steady heartbeat echoing in my head. Even after all that's happened, after seeing her face contorted in absolute evil, she looks so peaceful in slumber. Unable to let her go, I lie beside her and pull her into my arms, placing her head on my chest. The feeling of holding another person, cradling them with such care and affection is foreign, but not unpleasant.

No. It's fucking perfect.

Amelie wraps her arm around my waist, rubbing her cheek against my chest. She lets out a soft sigh that ends in a hum. "Mmmm," she smiles. "Niko."

Come again?

I study her face to ensure that she is actually still asleep. Her breathing is deep and steady and her eyelids are sealed. I knew she was dreaming of me, but I'd never heard her say my name. And the smile attached to it? Shit. I feel like I just died a thousand sweet deaths.

All night, I hold Amelie tight as if she might slip away. And the truth is, she might. Something else - something deeply evil and unnatural - has corrupted her body. It has blackened her soul and claimed those startling, amber irises. I just hope to be strong enough to claim her heart.

IGHT

"So…what do you think?"

Blood red, beady eyes narrow speculatively. I know this is bad. It won't end well for Amelie… or me.

"Definitely sounds like she's possessed," Cyrus replies, rubbing the patch of dark hair on his chin. He scans the dimly lit bar for eavesdroppers before slipping his shades back on. Not that anyone would be alarmed; it's a Dark owned and operated establishment.

"But the shit with the Light … how do you explain that?"

"The Light in her is fighting against it. But whatever is in her - whatever evil is running through her veins - it's strong. Especially to manifest like that."

We both sit in silence, sipping our poison while mulling over Cyrus's theory. A few more patrons enter as night falls. Darkness brings the beasts to life.

"Who else have you told about her…" He looks around to ensure no one is overtly interested in our conversation. "…about her heritage?"

"No one," I answer, shaking my head. "I haven't told anyone but you."

"Because you know what that would mean for her."

He doesn't have to say it. I know exactly what Amelie's fate would be. What it *still* could be.

"And she had no recollection of that night?"

I shake my head. "She didn't remember a thing. However, she did mention a dream she had … said it scared her."

Cyrus looks over the rim of his dark shades, red eyes gleaming with blood lust. "Go on."

I take a deep breath, not wanting to say it out loud. I know how it must sound. Shit, it sounds suspect as hell even in my head. "She dreamt that I was on the ground, surrounded in a pool of blood, dying. And she … she was standing above me, apparently my murderer."

"Shit," Cyrus mumbles.

"Yeah." I down the rest of my bourbon and signal for another. "So honestly, what's your take on it? What should I do?"

I can see Cyrus's brows rise even behind his sunglasses. "You care about her, don't you?"

I lower my eyes to the wooden tabletop. "More than my dumb ass should."

"Hmph," he snorts. He tips back the rest of his blood infused whiskey. "I'll head back to Skiathos. Do some digging. In the meantime, you do what she told you."

My eyes lift to meet his knowing grin. Although it's not intended, it makes him look all the more menacing against his fangs. "What?"

"You do what she told you to do. You help her. You save her." He smiles wide for added effect, and I see just a tiny glimpse of the roguish brute from my childhood. "You love her."

"I don't know," I say shaking my head, though I can't hide my own grin. "I don't know if it's possible."

"But whatever you do," he adds sternly in a hushed voice. "You don't tell another soul about her. I'm serious, Niko. Do you know what your enemies will do with that kind of information? That's like handing over a loaded gun."

"I know. I know that, Cy. But how do I protect her? And what makes you think that she even feels anything for me?"

"She sleeps beside you every night, right?"

"Yeah."

"And she's no longer spelled to the room?"

"Right."

"Then I don't think," he remarks, certainty resonating through his deep, husky voice. "I know."

The house is in full swing later that evening, the depraved and wicked hungry for another taste of the taboo. The night is unseasonably warm for autumn, and the electrical charge in the air sends prickly heat all over my skin. This is no ordinary evening. It's Halloween, and that means more than just ghouls, goblins and candy for kids. The Dark are out to play.

I make my way up to my room, dodging fake spider webs, bed sheet ghosts and other gaudiness. The girls have had their fun decorating, and now they will earn their keep. Everyone is just a little more susceptible, more *open* on Halloween.

Amelie isn't in my room, and something in my gut twists. I want to tell her how I feel. Tell her that I care for her and will do anything to protect her. Tell her that having her work as a sexified housekeeper was just my immature way of keeping her close to me. Then, I'll hope like hell she feels something for me. Something strong enough to make the beautiful maiden stay with the beast.

I pour a glass of bourbon, but it never meets my lips. It's smashed against the wall in a million tiny shards, auburn liquor pooled on the floor. I'm looking into bright, azure eyes, my teeth clenched and my lips tight in fury. A chill sweeps over my body, igniting the white-hot flame in my fingertips. My eyes glow, fueled by unmistakable rage.

"You have thirty seconds to explain what you're doing in my room before I rip your fucking head off and punt that shit back to Skiathos." My hand tightens around her neck, lifting her off of her 5-inch heels.

"Good to see you too, Niko," Aurora smiles through the pain in her neck. "I can see you've missed me. Quite a welcoming party you have here."

I squeeze tighter. "Twenty seconds, bitch."

Her blue eyes flash with her own anger, but her shit-eating grin remains. "I bring news. News about your brother that you need to know."

News? News about Dorian?

I drop her brusquely and turn back to the bar as she straightens her hair and clothing. "Fine. Talk."

"I'm doing great, thank you for asking. No, no need to thank me for coming all this way to share secret information with you that could have me beheaded," she says in her annoying singsong voice.

"Ok, now that pleasantries are out of the way, talk. Or leave." I down the glass in one gulp and pour another. I'm going to need a gallon to stomach my brother's conniving, manipulating ex.

"Such a shame, Niko. You had so much potential." She inspects her red painted nails, ignoring my command. "Now look at you. Nothing more than a pimp in an expensive suit."

"Do you really have information, Aurora? Or have you finally realized that you can get paid for being such a dirty slut?" I look her up and down, grimacing in disgust. Even designer clothes and all the accoutrements couldn't make her any less of a skank. "I don't know though. Your pussy has been run through more times than the Mulholland Tunnel. I guess I can keep you around for the occasional gang bang or farm animal."

She stalks toward me, wearing her usual sickly sweet smile, unfazed by my insults. Aurora only hears what she wants to hear, and in her mind, I'm probably professing my undying devotion. Crazy bitch.

"Oh, Little Skotos. You always did have a way with words."

See? Bat shit crazy.

"Well, read these words. Get. The. Fuck. Out." I give her my back, refusing to entertain her for one more second.

"Dorian has disappeared."

I turn and narrow my eyes. "What?"

"He's disappeared - he and his partner. Both of them AWOL from the Shadow. No one knows where either is and it's come to the point to expect the worst."

"He's not dead, Aurora." No. He can't be.

She shakes her head. "I don't believe he is either. But something is definitely wrong. What if he's been seriously injured and is being held prisoner? What if he's being tortured?"

Though her words are full of concern, her face, her eyes, tell a different tale. Aurora is as transparent as they come. She's fake … phony. She doesn't truly care about Dorian - she never did. She only cared about what his title could do for her. All Aurora saw was a crown.

"I'm worried," she continues with mock compassion. "I think your father could at least find out if he's been captured. They'd have to return him as a sign of diplomacy."

"Maybe," I shrug. "Why don't you ask him? Seeing as you know him intimately and all. Or did he fuck and forget you just like everyone else in your miserable life?"

Rage paints her cheeks, yet Aurora's guise is perfectly impassive. She's not just any gold-digging whore; she's a father-fucking, gold-digging whore. And because my father, the reigning king of the Dark, is just as disgusting, Dorian was forced to bear witness to the indiscretion.

"Oh? Cat caught your tongue?" I dig. "Or did blowing every Tom, Dick and Harry cause it to finally fall off?"

And I see it. The crack in her armor. That little flash of emotion that makes Aurora seem almost human.

Her hands shake at her sides as she steps toward me. "You know I couldn't help that! You know I-"

"Oh my God!" Amelie huffs out as she swings open the door, dressed in her skimpy French Maid outfit. "I am so sick of those-"

"Who the fuck is this?" Aurora sneers, venom dripping from her bright white teeth. "Is this how the whores behave around here?"

Amelie looks at me for guidance, mouth agape and those amber eyes full of question. Fuck. Was I so hell-bent on slighting Aurora that I couldn't even sense her approach?

"Aurora, this is Amelie, and she's not a whore," I explain with a flat voice. "Amelie, Aurora was just leaving."

"Just leaving?" Aurora asks, cutting her eyes at me, then back to Amelie. "No. We still have business to discuss, so if you'll excuse us..."

I can see Amelie's hurt and anger brewing just under the surface, making her even easier to detect. I have to get Aurora out of here. If she even catches wind of Amelie's unique touch of magic, she won't hesitate to slaughter her. And killing another member of the Dark, especially an Orexis, is highly frowned upon.

"How about I meet you downstairs for a drink, Aurora?" I say in my most amenable voice. "Just let me have a word with Amelie and I'll join you soon."

Aurora's skeptical eyes sweep between both Amelie and me before nodding. "Fine. But don't take too long. I don't like to wait." Then she struts out the door without so much as a second glance.

"Wow," Amelie remarks, closing the door behind her. "Who was that ray of sunshine?"

I exhale my relief that Amelie isn't totally put off by me being here alone with Aurora. In three quick strides, I'm in front of her, letting the warmth of her soul heat the frigid space that Aurora has left behind.

"My brother's psychotic ex-girlfriend. Quite the charmer, isn't she?"

"The one that made him skip town? That ex-girlfriend?"

"One and the same."

Amelie shakes her head. "Can't say that I blame him."

We both share a chuckle at Aurora's expense when I see Amelie wince. That's when I notice a small, purplish bruise at the corner of her mouth. "What happened?" I ask, moving in to inspect the slightly swollen spot.

"Speaking of Sunshine…you may want to put a muzzle on your blonde bitch," she says rolling her eyes.

"What happened?" I ask more sternly.

Amelie shrugs it off. "It's nothing, really. Just another day at

Hooker High. Sunshine kept running her mouth about me getting special treatment and how I must be into some sick shit to have gotten your attention. I doubt she'll be saying much of anything for a while. Sorry, but she'll be off blowjob duty for at least a week," she says with a wink.

"She hit you?" I snap, fury lighting my eyes.

"Did you not hear the part about me whooping her ass? It's cool, Niko. I've had to deal with bigger bitches than her back home."

I try to tame the feelings of frustration and helplessness as I gaze into Amelie's eyes, searching for some sign that she's really ok. Lifting a hand, I gently brush the contusion with my fingertips, eliciting a groan from her.

"I'm sorry, did I hurt you?"

Before I can pull my hand away, she covers it with hers. "No. No, it feels good, actually. You're always so cold. Like my own personal ice pack," she smiles.

I revel in the feeling of her lips against my fingers, the subtle burn almost nonexistent, though there is indescribable heat between us.

"I can help you, you know," I say quietly, my hand still pressed to her luscious mouth. I don't want to stop touching her. I can't see myself touching anyone else for the rest of my days.

"How?" she whispers.

A blue haze falls over her face and reflects in her eyes as my fingers alight with iridescent, azure fire. She flinches at the initial cold before giggling against my hand. "It's so … odd. Cold, but hot. And it's tingly."

"Yeah," I reply, with a goofy grin. It's the first time I've ever let myself be exposed like this with a human. "I guess it's a testament to the Dark. We're cold, callous, yet hot tempered and explosive when agitated."

Amelie shakes her head, but still keeps her hand on mine, refusing to break contact. Warmth kindles and spreads all over my body. "Not all the Dark. Not you."

We stare at each other in silence, soft smiles on both our lips, as I gently rub the bruise on Amelie's face. "What are you doing to it?" she asks in wonder.

"Just accelerating blood flow in the area and numbing the pain for you."

"It doesn't hurt that bad."

I shrug, only the taste of truth resting on my tongue. "I don't ever want you to be in pain. Not even the slightest bit."

Amelie's cheeks burn with a rosy flush and she sucks her lower lip into her mouth, capturing it between her teeth. "So … you're healing me?"

"I can't heal," I say shaking my head in regret. "Just simple science."

"There's nothing simple about this. I don't even feel it anymore. You're incredible, Niko."

I realize that I have been studying her pink lips for longer than I should and lift my eyes to meet hers, only to find that she's looking at my lips as well. Our eyes lock, both our mouths parting simultaneously to taste the air between us, tinged with longing and desire.

"Did I make you too numb?" I ask in a husky voice.

Amelie wiggles her mouth adorably and shakes her head. "I don't think so. Why?"

Only inches lie between our mouths as I look into those peculiar eyes, wondering how I ever survived without feeling Amelie's warmth and goodness. And how I ache to taste sunlight and wildflowers and brown sugar on my tongue.

"Because I really want you to feel this."

Our mouths collide in a fevered blur of lips, tongues and hands. This isn't one of the fairytale kisses you read about in storybooks. Not the pretty puckers in chick flicks. It's raw passion combined with weeks of yearning and wanting. It's going into unknown territory, terrified of what might be on the other side, but so fucking exciting to do so. It's embracing taboo, tasting forbidden fruit, and relishing in its sweet, sweet nectar.

Kissing Amelie ignites fireworks in my belly and makes the cold deadness of my heart bloom with life. I didn't know that lips could feel this soft. That a tongue could taste so delectable. That her delicate hands could feel so damn erotic as they slip through my hair, pulling my mouth closer. That's why I hadn't kissed anyone in decades. There was no need to be that intimate with anyone. No need to stage a charade when I knew sex was inevitable anyway.

But Amelie…*Fuck*.

I didn't want to stop kissing her. I couldn't imagine not having her taste on my tongue. The little sounds of ecstasy she made in her throat as I caressed her petite frame had me aching for more, yet this was enough. It was more than enough.

Feeling her soft curves so pliant under my eager fingertips, imagining how truly fragile she was, made me feel like I possessed a rare, precious jewel. I wanted to touch her all over. To mark her in places that no other man could see. To be the only man that would ever feel the softness of her skin.

Minutes, hours, eternity tick by as we stand enraptured in each other's arms. She looks up at me, a coy smile on her now swollen lips.

"What's that look for?" I ask, wearing the same expression.

"Nothing," she grins, shaking her head. "Just thinking how that was so much better than my dreams."

I exhale, desperately wishing I could stay in this moment with her. To remain oblivious to the killers, whoremongers and degenerates who lurk right outside our bedroom door.

"As much as I would love to stay here and play out all those dreams, I know Aurora is getting impatient. And when she's impatient, she's even more of an annoying trollop. I gotta go down and see what she wants. Then … then I'm all yours."

Even as the words leave my lips, I can't even believe I'm saying them. I'm good with words, but there's usually some vulgar connotation attached to them. *Spread your legs. Look at me while I fuck you. Suck harder, deeper.* And my personal favorite: *Get up and get the fuck out.*

But with Amelie, I couldn't even say that stupid shit even if I wanted to. And that's the thing - I don't want to. Even thinking about it makes me sick to my stomach.

"Ok," she smiles, looking up at me though long dark lashes. "I'll just get cleaned up. Maybe run down to the kitchen and grab us some dinner?"

I press my lips against her forehead, inhaling the intoxicating scent of her hair. "That sounds perfect." And miraculously, it does.

I make my way down to the parlor to find Varshaun and Aurora huddled in a hushed exchange while Nadia and a few of my men make small talk over drinks. Varshaun's cunning, azure eyes gleam with mischief as he frowns at Aurora. She grazes his arm with familiarity, and moves in closer to whisper something in Dark tongue - something too fast for me to hear.

Feeling the heat of my glare, Varshaun jerks his head and brushes her hand from his forearm. "So nice of you to join us, Niko," he smiles slyly. "Seems like you've been holed up in your suite for weeks. We hardly ever see you."

"Oh?" Aurora retorts, her voice dripping with phoniness.

"Ah, Niko has a new toy. And if I were him, I'd play with her all the time too," Nadia adds, sidling beside me. She hands me a fresh glass of my favorite bourbon before kissing my cheek, her bright blue eyes sparkling with affection. She loves me. Not as a lover, but as a friend. A sibling. For decades, Nadia has been an instrumental part of my team, caring for the girls I employ, and even enjoying them herself, on occasion.

"Well, let's just hope he doesn't break this one!" Varshaun jibes with boisterous laughter.

I roll my eyes, hoping to thaw my annoyance and conjure the warmth that swept through me just minutes before. Even as they laugh and joke at my expense, all I can think about is Amelie. I want to feel that burn on my lips, stoke the fire with my eager hands. Kiss the sun and let its brilliance blind me until all I can do is bask in her gentle smile.

"Well, maybe Niko will let us all play with his new, little pet," I hear Aurora suggest, turning to Varshaun. He shakes his head.

"Believe me, I've tried. But he's not done having his fun just yet. I think we'll wear him down soon enough," he replies with a wink.

I'm just about to open my mouth to … shit. What would I say? How can I tell them to back the hell off without jeopardizing my stance as their ruthless, philandering prince? And without dispelling the rouse and revealing who I truly am and what I truly want?

I look around at the jovial faces, talking over crystal glasses of fine bourbon and wine. Outside of Aurora, these are the people I have spent everyday with for the last several decades with. *My so-called friends.* They don't know me. None of them do. Not even Nadia who genuinely cares for me like her own family. Not even Varshaun who has been my wingman and right hand for longer than a human lifetime. We've fought together, killed together … hell, we've even fucked together. Still, he has no clue of the conflict boiling right beneath surface. He doesn't know that I struggle with this…with what I am. He doesn't know that most days, I dance with death only to feel some semblance of life. That my hunger for power is as deep and real as is my guilt and shame.

"Don't tell me Little Skotos has gotten attached," Aurora jibes, placing a perfectly manicured hand on my chest. "Not the guy that screwed over half the continental US during the 60s. Surely they're mistaken."

I flash a devilish grin and lift a dark brow, ready to defend my sullied reputation when movement from over Aurora's head catches my eye. Amelie's eyes are wide and shining with unshed tears, her perfect mouth in a tight line. A tray of food visibly shakes in her trembling hands. Following my line of vision, Aurora turns her head slowly, her cold, piercing gaze sweeping the length of Amelie's body. She turns back to me, wearing a mocking grin, awaiting my reaction.

"Ah, Little Skotos, looks as if the whores are getting comfortable around here. You may need to crack the whip a bit harder. Which I'm sure you'll enjoy."

I clutch Aurora's hand hard enough for the bones to crack and remove it from my shirt. She winces as my eyes meet hers, my steely glare blazing with ire. "There's nothing *little* about me, Aurora. But of course, you wouldn't know that seeing as I've rejected every one of your feeble advances." I move in even closer, so close that the iciness of my voice damn near leaves frost on her diamond studs. "And if you ever call her a whore again, I'll cut your fucking tongue out and stuff it up your sagging pussy. Now if you'll excuse me…"

I brush past her without another word, striding in the direction of Amelie's retreating back. She nearly sprints to my room – to *our* room – before setting down the tray and turning to face me.

"Amelie, I…"

She holds up a hand and shakes her head. "Don't bother. You don't owe me an explanation. You don't owe me anything."

"But I do. I owe you more than I could ever give you. I owe you the truth."

"The truth?" Her brow furrows and she places a hand on her narrow hip. "I thought that's what you had been giving me this entire time. At least that's what you promised when I vowed to be totally truthful with you. So what? That was all a lie?"

I sit down at the foot of the bed and pat the empty space beside me. "I have. At least as honest as I could be. Please. Let me explain."

Amelie sits on the bed though two feet separate our bodies. A few weeks ago, that wouldn't have bothered me. But now … now that I know what it feels like to have her body tucked into mine, my arms encircling her small frame, possessing her, it feels too far away. I didn't even realize how much of a permanent fixture she had become in my life. How easy it was to fall into familiarity with her. How natural the burn underneath my fingertips had grown every time we touched. I crave it. It signifies the fire between us - the unmistakable heat that will never, ever die.

She draws her knees up against her chest and wraps her arms around them. Much like she did the first time she woke up in my bed. She's afraid. Afraid of *me*.

"I need to explain why I asked you if anyone knew about you. And why no one can know about us…about how I feel."

"How you feel?" Her voice is breathy and light, almost a whisper.

"Yes," I nod. "But I need to tell you something first. And if you still want to know more, I'll tell you. Ok?"

She nods and I take that as my cue to scoot closer beside her, taking her hands in mine. "Amelie, the Dark, the Skotos especially, have been sworn enemies of the Laveaus for decades. Many, many years ago, they ruled Louisiana. They were the most influential family in the gulf and held a great amount of power for human witches, something virtually unheard of. Throughout history, my kind has had to intervene when certain clans have grown too large or too powerful. But the Laveaus…they wouldn't back down, especially after Marie was eliminated. Her family - *your* family – vowed to avenge her death."

Amelie's large, sparkling eyes urge me to go on. I brush a lock of hair behind her ear before bringing her hands to my lips, inhaling shallowly. "At my father's command, we tried to kill them all. What history books call the Cheniere Caminanda Hurricane of 1893, the deadliest storm to ever plague Louisiana, was the work of the Dark. It was a deliberate massacre that killed even innocent women and children. The Laveaus had grown like a cancer, and the Dark fought to snuff them all out. However, some survived and went underground, so every few years, we do it again. Until every last one is gone."

A tiny whimper escapes her chest, and she claps a hand over her mouth, fighting tears. "No," she cries, her hand muffling her plea. "Don't say that. I won't believe it!"

I pull her into my chest and place my lips at the crown of her head, though she tries to fight against me. I just want to hold her. I *need* to. It may be the last time I ever kiss the sun. "I'm sorry, baby. I am. I didn't want to tell you. I didn't want to hurt you."

"Why? How could you?" Her tears flow freely, yet I resist the urge to taste them. I won't do that to her. I won't let her see what a sick fuck I truly am. "I don't understand. Help me understand why!"

"Housekeeping." I don't know any other way to say it. No matter how badly I want it to be a lie, the truth is as ugly and abhorrent as it has ever been. And it's *my* truth. *My* ugliness.

"Can you stop it?" she asks, looking up at me with pleading eyes. "Please, innocent people are dying. Their homes, their lives! You can fix this, right?"

"I wish I could. I was sent here to monitor paranormal activity in the area. Anytime there is a rise in the use of magic, it's my job to report it. So we can prepare…"

"…To kill more people. To destroy my city." She pulls away from me and gives me her back.

"I need your help, Amelie."

"My help?" She spins to glare at me, those amber eyes gleaming with anger. "You want me to help you? After you just admitted to sending hurricanes to demolish my home?"

"Yes," I nod, swallowing around a knot in my throat. "Because if you don't, something will happen. Something bad. And if you help me, we can avoid more destruction."

"Fine," she huffs out. "Tell me what you need."

I take a deep breath, reluctant to conjure memories of Amelie's face distorted in repugnance. "There's been a surge in magic. Necromancy to be exact. And it reeks of Laveau Voodoo. Necromancy itself is grounds for action…for mass extermination."

I wait for her to object, but she just continues to stare at me, the warmth in her eyes extinguished. I continue. "The other night, while you were sleeping, you had a nightmare. I tried to wake you because you were frightened, and when I did, something – someone - had taken over your body. It had possessed your soul and tongue. It spoke to me."

"Wha … what? Possessed? What are you talking about?"

"Black magic, Amelie. The Laveaus know that I have you. And something tells me that they want to use you as a vessel, to have you do their bidding."

"That's crazy talk," she refutes, shaking her head.

"Amelie, listen to me," I command, grasping her shoulders. "They are willing to sacrifice you to exact revenge. They know you'll be slaughtered and they don't give a damn. I won't let that happen, Amelie. I swear it. I can't lose you. Now that I've found you … I can't lose you."

Her lips tremble as she brushes my cheek with her palm. "Ok. I believe you. Just tell me what I need to do."

I tell her more about necromancy and its history among the Laveaus. I share with her the clues left around town, even information only my inner circle is made aware of. She listens intently, nodding, trusting me as I trust her. I tell her everything, even the parts that cause my chest to ache with shame. She listens, squeezing my hand, and looking at me with understanding and forgiveness.

I don't deserve this girl. I'll never earn the right to hear her laughter or to possess the goodness of one of her smiles. Or to feel those soft lips caressing mine. Even knowing this, I want her. I need her.

We lay side-by-side like we do every night, facing each other as the trees outside my window cast shadows across her face.

"You never did tell me how you feel," she whispers, her eyes heavy with exhaustion.

"Do you want me to tell you now?"

"No," she replies with a small yawn. "No, you don't have to tell me. Just show me."

I close the inches between us and wrap her in my arms, burying my lips in her wildflower-scented hair. She snuggles into my chest and sighs. I can feel every bone in her body relax in slumber.

I'll show her. I'll save her. Because I love her.

NINE

"Where are we going?"

I look over from the driver's seat and wink, causing a blush to paint Amelie's cheeks. "You'll see. Patience, love."

"Fine," she replies, folding her arms across her chest. "Would have been nice if you would've at least told me how to dress. I must look ridiculous sitting in such an expensive car, looking like a pauper."

"Nonsense," I reply. And I mean it. Even dressed in tight jeans and a loose fitting sweater, Amelie looks incredible sitting in the passenger seat of my vintage Ferrari. She shrugs, and the sweater slides off one of her shoulders, revealing bare, mouthwatering skin. I don't even think twice before I reach over to run my fingers from her collarbone to her arm, making her shiver. "Absolutely beautiful."

"You're insane," she giggles. "You're around naked chicks every single day. They're ready to spread 'em on command. I know I'm no ogre, but, hell, sex appeal is not really in my repertoire." She shrugs again, and the sweater slips down further, exposing the swell of one full, naked breast. Fuck. She isn't wearing a bra.

"Are you trying to make me lose my damn mind and crash my favorite car? You have no idea how fucking sexy you are."

"Whatever."

"Seriously. I can't even describe it. Naked chicks are a dime a dozen in my profession. But you...you could make a burlap sack look obscene on your body."

She shakes her head and looks out the window. "It's fine, Niko. You don't have to lie. You forget that I know how you are. How often you...have sex. You aren't exactly subtle when it comes to that stuff. But with me...nothing. I mean, you're sweet, and gentle, and romantic, and I love all that stuff. But I know I must not turn you on *like that.* I've been sleeping beside you for weeks in skimpy nightgowns, and you haven't looked once."

I pull the car over into the parking lot of a pawn shop, and my lips are moving against Amelie's not even two seconds after the car is in park. My tongue tangles with hers in a rough, aggressive dance, desperate to taste every bit of her. When I pull away, I take her hand and mold it to hardness in my groin, drawing a gasp from her lips.

"Do you feel that? Do you see what you do to me? You did that, Amelie. It's you that has me so rock hard that I can barely think straight. You and only you. If this doesn't tell you how badly I want you, I don't know what will."

Amelie's face is beet red with a mixture of fiery passion and bashfulness. But even after I remove my hand from on top of hers, she still grips my dick, kneading it gently through my slacks. I let out a low hiss between my teeth and let my head fall back on the seat.

"Damn, Amelie. Touch me, baby," I rasp, my voice thick with lust.

Amelie licks her lips before running her fingers over my entire length. Her eyes dance with excitement and hunger, and I can hear her heartbeat pound faster with every timid stroke. The heat of her hand seeps through the fabric of my pants, causing the throb to evolve into an ache. I reach over and run my thumb along her lush bottom lip. The very tip of Amelie's pink tongue darts out to taste it.

The fire in her eyes, the scent of her arousal that flavors the air between us, her blood racing in her veins with anticipation... I know that Amelie wants this. She wants *me.* Even after everything I've told her, everything she's seen flash across her subconscious when she closes her eyes, she's still drawn to me like a moth to a flame. Her nipples harden underneath the veil of her sweater, free and unrestricted without the coverage of a bra. Her breath quickens as she feels me pulsing underneath her fingertips. Her mouth waters as she imagines my taste, my feel.

I could give her what she wants, right here and now in this abandoned parking lot. I could recline her seat and bury myself in her tight body and make those dreams a reality. But I won't. Amelie is better than that, and she deserves more than some quick fuck in my car. She deserves tenderness and care. She deserves for me to love her heart and mind, as well as her body.

"We should get going," I mutter, hating the words even as I say them. I gently grasp her hand and bring it up to my lips, kissing every fingertip before placing it in her lap. Amelie lets out a half groan in response, or maybe in protest, of losing the heaviness of my erection in her hand. Still, I turn and force my eyes back on the road, though I'm almost dizzy with wanting her so damn bad.

Several minutes later, we pull up to a wrought iron gate located in the outskirts of town. Luckily, blood flow has returned to my extremities and I'm able to focus on punching in the key code and maneuvering my way down the long, winding dirt path.

"Where are we?" Amelie asks, seeing the makings of a large plantation-style home through the trees.

I wait until the entire grand estate is in view, before answering. "My house."

Amelie's eyes grow large and bright with wonder. "This is your house? You live here?"

"Yeah," I answer, guiding the car around the fountain in the driveway before coming to a halt. I glance at her awestruck expression as she takes it all in. "Wanna see the rest?"

Amelie nods excitedly. "Yes! Yes, please."

Before she draws her next breath, I'm outside her door, clicking it open and offering her my hand. She shakes her head, and takes it, a playful smile on those perfect, crimson lips. "Show off," she teases.

We make our way up the stairs and through the front door, entering the grand foyer that's immaculately decorated with artwork and tapestries from as early as the Renaissance. Amelie is nearly giddy with curiosity, her eyes and hands eager to explore every inch of the Greek Revival home.

"If you have this house, why the hell do you stay in the city? I mean, it's nice there too, and nearly as large, but this place … this is spectacular."

I shrug although I know she can't see me, as she studies one of the many paintings. "Honestly? It's more convenient to stay in the city. I need to stay on top of things to ensure everyone is taken care of. Plus … I don't want to be alone. Even amongst all these treasures, the house seems empty. Lonely. And I hate it."

Amelie turns to face me, sympathy etched in her soft features. "You're not alone." She squeezes my hand and smiles, filling me with comforting warmth. "Even before you even knew I existed, I was with you. A spectator, but I was with you just the same."

I pull her into my arms, yet stop just before our lips meet. "Why are you so good to me? How can someone so beautiful care for a monster like me?"

"You're not a monster. No matter what you are, you could never be a monster."

I kiss her like she'll disappear in a puff of smoke. As if she is a mythical creature, birthed into an ugly world of disease and pain, sent here to bring beauty to the devastation. Sent here to smother the dark desolation with brilliant, golden light.

"I want to show you the house," I breathe, my lips still brushing hers. "But I have to admit, all I'm thinking about is the bedroom."

She giggles and nuzzles her nose against mine. "You've had me all to yourself in a bedroom for weeks. Show me your palace, my prince."

I give her the grand tour, opting to leave the master suite for later. I know that once I lock her in there, she'll never leave, not if I have anything to say about it. We end sometime later in the kitchen.

"The staff is off for the weekend but my cook left some food for us," I say, opening up the refrigerator and removing a wrapped platter. "Hungry?"

"I'm always hungry," Amelie replies with a wicked grin. The

possibility that her appetite is for something else entirely causes my dick to twitch and I almost drop the dish of assorted meats, cheeses and olives. Shit. How long has it been? Weeks? A month? How am I even able to walk straight?

We sit at the marble-top island, talking and laughing over finger food and wine while watching the sunset through the floor to ceiling windows, wall-size windows.

"This is amazing," Amelie breathes, as the setting sun casts hues of pinks and oranges across her face. "I don't understand why you would ever leave this place. It's like a museum, but it feels like … home."

I reach out to grasp her hand, drawing her attention to my earnest expression. "I wouldn't, if I had a reason to stay."

"This beautiful home would be reason enough for me," she shrugs.

"I'm glad you said that. Because that's exactly what I'm hoping for."

A cute little crease dimples her forehead in confusion. "What do you mean, Niko?"

I circle the kitchen island to stand before her, placing my hands on the curve of her hips. "I want you to come here to live, so I can be assured that whatever may come for me, you'll be safe."

Her eyes search mine for some sign of jest. "And what about you?"

"I'll keep looking for answers, hoping that whatever happened the other night was a fluke. But I need to focus, and I can't even think of anything but you when you're near. Having you at the manor … that's not a place for you. You belong in beauty, not surrounded by filth. You deserve to dance in the light, not condemned to the dark."

"Then … no." Amelie shakes her head and eases off the barstool, turning to leave the kitchen.

"No?" I ask, following her through the dining area.

"No. I'm not staying here." She turns to face me, her eyes bright and sparkling with conviction. "Not without you. After everything I've been through - being ripped from my home, thrown into a freakin' whorehouse, not to mention, all without an ounce of concern from my father who's probably drank himself to death by now - the only thing I've come to rely on is you. I've slept next to you for weeks. I've seen you in my dreams a million times. You are the only constant in my life. You are the only reason I am even able to sleep every night. Because no matter what the hell you are and what you've done, you were placed in my life for a reason. And dammit, I was placed in yours. So don't you dare…don't you dare try to leave me like everyone else."

I brush away the tears that have begun to slide down her cheeks. Eyes locked on her, I ease my thumb into my mouth and suck the salty moisture, drawing a gasp from her parted lips. I don't stop there. I taste them all, placing open-mouthed kisses on every tear, soothing her anguish with tenderness, care…and love.

"I won't leave you, baby," I whisper between kisses. "I'll always be with you. Always."

I kiss her heated cheeks, her soft, lush lips, and the angle of her jaw. Yet, it's not enough. Not enough to sate the hunger inside me.

"I need to kiss you all over," I whisper, before running my tongue along the shell of her ear.

"Ok," she breathes, her pert nipples brushing against my chest.

I lift my head and meet her sultry gaze. I need to know. I need to know that she's certain. "Ok?"

"Ok," she nods slowly, almost painfully. "I want you."

I give her my lips, my tongue, my hands … me. Anything and everything to show her that I want her too, more than I've ever wanted anyone. When our mouths finally part, we're in the master bedroom, surrounded by the soft glow of candlelight.

Amelie steps back, taking her warmth with her. Discontentment begins to flood my chest, but before the storm ensues, she smiles. Smiles at me like I'm *somebody* to her. Somebody special, deserving of her affection. The only *somebody* in this entire world that she wants to be with at this very moment, alone in this room.

I can't wait another second, although my head is screaming at me to slow down and take my time. But shit… I've been waiting two fucking centuries to feel this way. To feel *something.*

I step forward and grip the hem of her sweater, searching for any sign of doubt. But to my surprise and delight, Amelie lifts her arms above her head, and I am only too eager to comply. My fingers whisper across her waist and ribcage as I draw the fabric up and over her head. Before the sweater can even hit the floor, my lips are already aching to taste her luminescent skin.

"Amelie." It comes out as a plea … a whimper. Because, *fuck,* she's too beautiful. It almost hurts to be in the presence of something so magnificent. I want to touch her, but for some reason, I don't. I can't. My eyes can only devour the expanse of her flat belly, the round heaviness of her breasts, and the delicateness of her collarbone. I've never been like this. Shit, I know the female form inside out. But the sheer wonder of Amelie's body has left me speechless. Fucking speechless.

Almost as if she hears my emotions battling against my hormones, Amelie steps forward and takes my hand in hers. Agonizingly slow and gentle, she brings it to rest on her chest, right over the vital space that houses her heart. The very same place I touched days ago when I contemplated ripping it from her body to end her life. And now, as I feel her heart beat rapidly, the heat of her skin sizzling the surface of mine, I feel as if I have been reborn. Numb and blind for two hundred years, she has just pulled me out of perpetual darkness.

She looks up at me, those peculiar eyes gleaming with longing. "Touch me. Please."

The fact that she even feels the need to beg has me hating myself. My fingers slide down her torso, taking in the silkiness of her skin, before rising up to meet her breasts. We both groan as I cup them, the nipples hardening against my palm.

"Baby, you…you are…" Shit, I'm a blubbering mess. I rub my

thumbs across her nipples before giving her swollen breasts a squeeze. So soft. So fucking soft. "You are…perfect."

My lips find hers, my tongue seeking entrance to her mouth, as I explore her body with my hands, the burn coupling with the unrelenting throb in my slacks. I could do this all night. I could be placated with just kissing and touching her like this. But I won't. I need more of Amelie. I need all of her.

My fingers travel down to her jeans, and I slowly undo the clasp, giving her ample time to stop me. She doesn't. She only tightens the grip on my hair, as she deepens the kiss.

When her pants lie in a heap next to her shirt after she's kicked them off in eagerness, I stand back and admire the prize before me bare, unsullied and unashamed. Amelie. *My* Amelie.

I swallow, but my mouth goes dry. "I said I wanted to kiss you all over, and I fully intend to. But I need to know … is this what you want? Because once you give yourself to me, you're mine forever. Once I feel you shake beneath me, every one of your trembles will belong to me. Once you call out my name, no other man's name will fall on your lips in passion. I won't be able to stand it, Amelie. I'll kill someone before they get the chance to see what I'm looking at right now. I swear it. You're too fucking beautiful for anyone else. Shit, you're too beautiful for *me*."

I don't even notice that my fists are shaking until Amelie steps forward to still them. "Yours, Niko. I've been yours for a decade already. Forever is easy."

We kiss with a fevered hunger that has us both panting by the time the bed meets the back of her legs. I ease her down gently and just take a moment to admire the view. She smiles up at me sweetly. "You know, it's kinda hard to kiss me when you're way up there. And it doesn't seem fair that you're still dressed, and I'm pretty much on display here."

"Then tell me what you want me to do."

Amelie licks her lips before pinning me with her own naughty glare, and my dick goes from rock hard to granite. "Take your clothes off."

I do as she wishes, starting with my shirt. Amelie watches with rapt fascination, the scent of her arousal growing stronger and thicker with every button. By the time I undo my pants, she's squirming and her skin is on fire.

I lay beside her, and we stare at each other, both completely exposed, unable to hide. We see it all - our sins, our virtues. The monsters that live inside us, and the ghosts of our pasts. And, as open as Amelie is for me, I am just as open to her - completely at her will, at her mercy.

"Now what?" I ask, my voice husky.

Amelie swallows down her fear and apprehension. "Kiss me."

"Where?"

"All over," she breathes. "Anywhere. Everywhere."

And I do just that, starting with her throat, resisting the urge to breathe in her sweet essence. Pleasure. This is all about her pleasure. And for once in my life, that's enough. I trail a path to her breasts, licking the outer mounds. When my tongue worships her nipple, Amelie cries out, and her fingers dig into my shoulders. I draw it entirely in my mouth and suck, causing her body to convulse.

"Careful, love," I say, smiling against her skin. "I've only just started."

She whimpers something unintelligible and I continue the delicious torment - sucking, licking and nibbling every mouthwatering bit of her as I slowly work my way down her stomach to the tops of her thighs. When I ease her legs apart, she gasps.

"Is this ok?" I ask.

I feel her body tense, but she nods. "Yes."

Thank. Fuck. After seeing the pure perfection between Amelie's thighs, covered in only a neat strip of dark hair, there's no way I can resist now. I've seen it. Smelled it. And now, I need to taste it.

I part her gently, feeling her slickness on my fingertips. I start at the insides of her thighs, kissing each tenderly while my thumb still rubs against her clit. She's wet, but I know it'll take patience and care to get her as wet as I need her.

"Oh God!" she cries out, her quivering building into convulsions. Wetness seeps from her entrance and I rub it into the sensitive clit. She's on the edge, ready to let go. Just as the flood ensues, I slip a finger inside her, and she comes, her tight walls clamping down on the digit. I feel every shudder, every pulse, as she moans my name, submitting to me.

I lower my mouth to her, lapping the sweetness that flows from her, my finger still tucked deep inside her pussy, moving in and out, fucking her, opening her. The erotic sounds she makes coupled with her taste have my head spinning and dizzy with expectation.

"You taste so good," I groan, my mouth buried in her pink folds.

"Yeah?" she asks, breathless.

"Yeah." I remove my finger, slick with her juices and offer it to her. "Taste."

Her mouth falls open in wonder, her eyes heavy with pleasure. "I can't do that."

"No?" I smile, easing the finger inside my mouth. "Fine, more for me." I really let loose then, licking her, sucking her, fucking her with my tongue. I slip in a finger while my mouth teases her clit. Then two fingers plunge inside her, stretching her walls, preparing her for my size. Her legs quiver on my shoulders, and her back and ass arch off the bed.

"Oh God! Oh Niko! I'm, oh my God, I'm..." she screams, and again, her sweet nectar meets my tongue, and I greedily drink every drop.

Her body is covered with a light sheen of sweat, and her breath is ragged when I climb up her body to kiss her lips. My fingers still move inside her slowly, milking her orgasm, and opening her even more. She trembles against my body.

"Niko," she whines against my mouth, her insides still pulsing with aftershocks. "That was...you are...*uh!*"

My cock lies against her thigh, throbbing with virility and harder than it's ever been. Amelie's petite hand reaches between us and grasps it, causing my whole body to go rigid. I groan as she begins to run her fingers over my length. Even with her inexperience, it feels good. Every touch, every stroke, feels like heaven.

"That's right, baby. Just like that," I rasp, thrusting into her palm.

Together, we fuck each other with our hands. My fingers stretch her pussy and plunge deeper and deeper while, she fists my dick from root to tip, her movements growing more confident. When we're both flush with need for more, I slowly move to position myself between her legs.

"Is this what you want?" I ask, looking down at her with concern.

"Yes," she nods. "I've wanted it for so long …"

I frown. "You have?"

Amelie nods and cups my cheek. "Seeing you with all those women, seeing what a skilled lover you are … I wanted that. I wanted to wear the same looks of pleasure as they did when you were inside them. I wanted it bad. I'd wake up and sometimes I'd…" She turns away, and her cheeks warm with embarrassment.

"Tell me," I whisper, turning her face back to mine. I ease down and take a nipple into my mouth, hoping to coax the truth out of her.

"Oooh," she moans. "Yeah, uh, mmmm…I'd wake up throbbing. And wet. I'd ruin my panties."

"Fuck," I say, imagining her so timid and disheveled with sleep, her pussy slick with desire. Desire for *me*. "That's so sexy."

"Yeah?"

"Yeah, baby." I remove my fingers from inside her, glistening with wetness. She watches as I spread her sweet juices all over her breasts, leaving them sticky with the evidence of her need for me. I lower my mouth to her swells and lick them clean, careful not to waste a drop.

"Now, *that's* sexy," Amelie says, her voice raspy.

I work my way up to her mouth, letting her taste herself on my tongue. She sucks it with eagerness, just as turned on by the act as I am. When the tip of my cock teases her entrance, she jerks, but doesn't stop me. Still, I pull away. I know she wants this, but for some reason, something inside me won't let me just plunge into her, and bury myself balls-deep inside those tight, wet walls. I've never experienced this ... restraint - this feeling of doubt. Amelie has been waiting for this moment for years. I have to make this good for her. I have to make this special.

"Wait." Just as the hurt begins to creep on her face, I brush my thumb against her swollen bottom lip and smile. "You've been dreaming of this for so long, baby. I want to make that dream come true. Tell me about it. Tell me what you want and I'll give it to you."

A blush paints Amelie's cheeks, and she shakes her head. "I can't. It's too embarrassing."

"I promise you, you have no reason to be embarrassed. We'll take it slow, ok? Tell me - am I on top of you, or are you on top?"

Amelie bites her lip and the blush deepens to a deep scarlet. "I'm on top," she whispers.

Before she can blink, she's straddling me as I lay beneath her on my back. Her heavy breasts bounce at the swift movement. "Done. What else?"

"Um, you're kinda sitting up. Your arms are around me and your face...your face is..." She looks down at her nipples that seem to harden on her unspoken command. Again, I position myself in a blur of movement, eager to do whatever she desires.

"And now?" I ask, sliding my hands up her back.

"And now...now you would grab my ass and lift me up, before easing me on top of you," she breathes, with a newfound, sexy confidence. "And you would suck my nipples and kiss me so I'm ready for you. And when you get all the way inside me, we'd hold each other tight, while we move together."

I stare at her with bewilderment, so willing to do as she pleases, yet almost afraid of disappointing her. As if sensing my reluctance, she slides my hands down to her ass, her own hands shaky and damp with nerves. And I realize that she's not the only one giving herself tonight. She isn't the only virgin. I may be the furthest thing from pure and virtuous, but I am offering something to Amelie that I have never given another. I am embarking on a monumental first, just as she is.

"Together, ok?" she whispers, kissing my lips. "We can do it together."

I nod and deepen the kiss, before trailing my tongue to her breasts. I suck hungrily, flicking the nipples in the way that makes her body shake and her pussy clench. She moans and pulls my hair, yet pushes my face deeper into her bosom. She rocks on my dick, slickening it with her wetness, telling me that she's ready.

Hell yes. Ready for *me.*

Gripping her ass, I lift her slowly, positioning her over my thick cock that stands tall and proud. I let the head tease her swollen entrance, and I can feel her insides already quivering.

"Look at me," I demand gently. Amelie complies, the topaz in her eyes gleaming brighter than I have ever seen. She smiles at me, and again, I feel like I am dancing on the sun. "You are so beautiful, baby. And I've waited too. I've been waiting for this too."

Agonizingly slow, I ease her down, thrusting upward slightly at the same time. Amelie cries out, and buries her face in the crook of my neck, her nails digging into my back. I pause.

"Look at me, baby." When Amelie complies, I see there are tears in her eyes. "We can stop if you want. We don't have to do this. Or...or let me help you. Let me take the pain away."

"No," she sobs, shaking her head. "I want this. And I want to feel all of you. The pain, the joy, the fear...all of you. I don't want to be numb for this. I want to feel all of you inside me."

Proving to me that she means every word, she resumes the slow descent onto my cock, her snug pussy nearly sucking me into her body. She grimaces with pain but doesn't stop, and honestly, I don't want her to. Even the inch of me that has torn through the barrier of tightness feels fucking incredible. Warm and wet, hugging me, squeezing me. I tangle my fingers in her hair and kiss her deep, inching up into her as she forces herself down. I swallow her cries of pain and replace them with whimpers of pleasure, as I tug her sensitive nipples.

We freeze in place, gazing at each other in wonder, as I pulse deep inside her. I want to move, but then again, I don't. I just want to savor this feeling of complete and utter happiness. I just want to remember every single detail and hang onto it forever. I can't explain it, but I know this very moment is pivotal. It's like I am supposed to mentally record these emotions running through me. I'm supposed to memorize the feeling of Amelie's body on top of mine, humid with sweat and heated desire. I am supposed to remember her scent of wildflowers and brown sugar mixed with a tinge of blood, signifying the gift she has given me. I am supposed to commit every moan, sigh and whimper to memory. I know it. I just don't know why I know it.

"I feel … so full," she whispers.

"Does it hurt?" I ask, bracing for her reaction.

"Yes. But it's not so bad anymore. It's nothing compared to how good it feels. How good *you* feel."

I slide my hands up and down her back, eager to touch every part of her inside as well as out. "I'm going to move, baby. You feel so fucking amazing; I need to feel more of you. Is that ok?"

"Yes, Niko," she nods, closing her eyes tight. "I want to feel more of you too."

I guide her hips in a slow grind, and we both moan, completely overwhelmed at how perfectly I fit inside her. Amelie is stiff at first, but as she stretches to accommodate me and the pain subsides, she begins to get into it, circling her hips and ass while pulling at my hair. My mouth never leaves her body, never tasting enough, feeling enough. I'm addicted to every droplet of sweat, just as I am addicted to her tears.

Heat snakes up my spine, shooting into my extremities. Every finger and toe tingles, every inch of my skin sizzles with delicious fire. This isn't the slight burn I feel when I touch Amelie's skin that has become so natural to me; this is something different entirely. It's an inferno of emotion, concentrated and converted into sensation. It floods my veins and attacks every nerve ending, making my whole body tremble with uncontrollable pleasure. The fire begins to burn hotter and brighter, building into a firestorm of unparalleled ecstasy.

We move together faster, harder, hungrier than ever before. Her clit rubs against my pelvic bone over and over, and Amelie's pussy clenches with every stroke. She's fucking me, taking me, possessing me. Making me hers forever.

The fire inside blazes out of control, and, before I can stop it, or contain it, it explodes. For the first time in years … decades … maybe even a century, *I* explode. Every muscle cries out, as I spill into Amelie, fighting her fire with my own. She's right there with me, clawing my back, as she tenses and convulses. Her pussy walls squeeze even tighter, drawing out my orgasm, refusing to let go. She pants and whimpers, and her body sags against mine in exhaustion and complete bliss.

When my muscles have finally unwound enough to move again, I lay us down, me on my back and Amelie on top of me, her body still connected with mine. I kiss the top of her head while my hands caress her sweat dampened back.

"Amelie," I breathe. Even after what we've shared, even after all our secrets have been told, saying her name is still a novelty to me. "Amelie, baby."

"Oui, Monsieur." She looks up at me, and smiles, her chin resting on her hands.

"How badly do you hurt? Are you sore?" I know I should keep this moment lighthearted, but shit, knowing that I hurt her, even in intimacy, fucks with me.

"Not sore enough to not want to do it again," she grins slyly. "But sore enough to know I should wait."

I lean forward and kiss her cute, little nose, and she giggles. "And yes, I want to do that again," she adds.

"Me too. Shit, truth be told, I could go again. But you need to heal. Next time, all I want you to feel is pleasure. No pain."

She smiles, but it doesn't meet her eyes. "Something the matter?" I ask, brushing her hair from her face.

Amelie shrugs, yet her eyes go glassy and distant. "It's just … in my dreams, whenever you were with other women, you did something. *Breathing*, I think you called it. And when you did, you looked so … so *hot*. And sexy. Like it felt good to you. And with me, you didn't. Like maybe there's something wrong with me? Or maybe it wasn't as good to you? I mean, I know it was my first time, and I'll get better, but I…"

I swallow her words in a kiss, refusing to let her speak such blasphemy. When we come up for air, I grasp her face in my hands. "Baby, I would never do that to you, and it has nothing to do with you not feeling good to me. Because Amelie, you do. You were amazing, baby. Breathing is a necessity for my kind. It's how we stay alive - by literally sucking the life out of others. I don't have to do that with you, and I won't, because you already brought me to life. With your smiles, your kisses, your laughter. I won't take an ounce of that away. It's what makes me…"

…love you.

The words are right there on the tip of my tongue, but I don't say them. I've never said them, not even to my parents. Not even to my brother, the only other person who deserved my affection. Love is not something the Dark speak freely about. We don't say it because we rarely feel it. And when we do, when we capture that rare and precious emotion, we lock it up tight and cherish it. We live for it. We die for it.

Placated with my explanation, Amelie rests her head on my chest, drawing circles with her fingers against my skin. "What's this say?" she asks, tracing the dark blue ink embedded over my heart.

"My last name. Skotos."

"It's beautiful." Then she leans over and kisses the Greek lettering that signifies my people … my sin. The mark that represents this monster of a man.

We both fall asleep some time later, with Amelie still nestled against my chest. And for the first time, after an immortal lifetime of starless skies and moonless nights, I dream.

EN

Something pulls me out of slumber in the middle of the night. I'm lying on top of the comforter where Amelie and I made love, yet she's not there in bed with me. She isn't lying on top of my chest or even curled against my side. No. She's standing beside me, her eyes ink black and completely shrouded with evil. Her arms are raised above her head, her hands holding a twelve-inch blade.

I roll away just as the knife comes plunging down, sinking hilt-deep into the mattress. Amelie looks at me, her face contorted unnaturally. "You will burn, demon. Everything you love will burn. Heed this warning: Vengeance will be mine."

She pulls the blade still speared in the mattress and raises it again. I know I can fight her off, but I don't want to. I don't want to hurt her. But right now, I'm not facing my Amelie, the girl that just gave me the most sacred part of her. The girl I have given the most sacred part of me. My Amelie is trapped somewhere inside herself, unable to break free. I have to save her. I *will* save her.

"Amelie, baby, wake up!" I shout. Only the width of the bed separates us, and I can see her – or *it* - trying to calculate a way around it. "I know you can hear me. Baby, you have to fight. You have to come back to me."

An inhuman screech bubbles from her chest, and the sinister voice laughs. "Your girl is lost forever, demon. She is as dead as you are."

Hearing those words awakens my own vicious beast, and cold sweeps over me, touching my fingertips and eyes. I can feel them transform as magic awakens inside me, and I tremble with the magnitude of its power.

"Leave her," I spit back, my voice as cold as the blue flames licking my hands and arms.

The voice cackles again, and a shiver snakes up my spine. She grips the blade as if she is about to lunge, and I raise my hands in preparation. But instead, she holds out her arm and sinks the edge into her forearm, spilling Amelie's dark red blood onto the floor and comforter.

Those black, desolate eyes find mine, and she smiles. "Everything you love will burn."

The knife clatters to the floor, and Amelie crumples in a dead heap. But before her head can hit the ground, I catch her and cradle her to my chest.

"Amelie! Amelie, talk to me, baby! Talk to me!" I shout, shaking her lifeless frame. Finally, she jerks awake, gulping oxygen, her wide eyes horrified. I thank the Divine, God, and every deity known to man.

"Oh my God!" she cries. She looks down at her arm, still gushing blood, and the knife just inches away. "What happened? What happened, Niko? What did I do?"

"Amelie, listen to me. Do you remember anything? Did you dream of something? Of someone? I need to know how to help you."

"No! I don't know what's happening to me! I don't know anything!"

Amelie wails into my chest, as I grab my discarded shirt nearby to wrap her arm in. It's still bleeding, and while I can numb some of the pain, I can't heal her. I need to get her medical attention.

"Baby, we have to go. I need to get back to the city so we can prepare. And you need a doctor."

I pick her up and carry her to the en suite bathroom. The faucet turns and fills the tub with warm, soapy water. I step inside with Amelie still in my arms.

"This is so not how I imagined our first bath together," she mumbles, as I cup water and pour it over her chest.

"I know. Not how I imagined it either, but this won't count. We'll get a redo. We deserve it."

I clean her tenderly, refusing to put her down. When my hand brushes her sex submerged in water, her breath catches and she groans. Gently, I part her folds, cleaning her carefully, however, I can't deny my hardness pulsing against her ass. Amelie smirks and wiggles, but instantly winces, and I know she is in too much pain to even think about sex right now.

Minutes later, we're dry, dressed, and headed back to New Orleans. This far from civilization, the road is pitch black but, of course, I see clear as day.

Amelie turns to me, sadness etched in those amber eyes. "I hate that this happened. I wanted it to be perfect. To be special. And now … now the dream is over."

I grip her hand between us, interlacing our fingers. "It was perfect. Outside of what happened to you, it was the best night of my life."

"Really?"

"Really. You are my dream, Amelie. It's not over. It's just the beginning."

By the time we arrive back in town, the feeling of warmth and serenity has been rekindled, and we fall into our usual easy exchange. It's not until I pull up to the house on Bourbon Street that a sense of sheer dread sweeps over me. Amelie looks over at me, her morbid expression telling me she feels it too.

"Something's wrong," she whispers.

"Yeah." I get out of the car and listen for any sign of malice from inside, yet everything is quiet. Too quiet. It's as if there is a spell around the house to contain noise. I try to communicate with someone – anyone – from inside, but there's a block. No one is strong enough to do something like that. No one except me.

I go around to Amelie's side of the car and open her door. "I want you to stay here. The key is in the ignition. If I'm not back in three minutes, I want you to drive. Drive as far as the car will take you. There's cash in the glove compartment. Just drive and you'll know when to stop. You'll know when you're safe."

"No," she cries, shaking her head. I'm not surprised; I knew she would object. "I'm not leaving you. Come with me. You don't have to go inside."

I stroke her hair before running a finger over her full bottom lip. "I do, baby. My people are in there. Those girls ... I swore to protect them. It could be nothing, and I'll probably be out here to get you in a few seconds. But I won't risk it. Just promise me you'll drive away, baby. I'll find you, I promise."

"You promise?" Tears streak down her cheeks, and I lean forward to kiss them away. Not for pleasure or to feed some sick, inner need, but to comfort her. To ease the trepidation that lies in her heart as well as mine.

"I promise."

I walk into the house, not knowing what to expect. I'm unsure of what lies in wait for me, what could be lurking behind a dark corner. But I know one thing for certain: Death is thick and heavy in the air. It's fresh, unforgiving and potent. I silently say goodbye to Amelie, knowing that in a few minutes, she will drive away from here. Away from the brutality that greets me in this place.

I scan the foyer, expecting to see bodies scattered about, but all is clear. Nothing is out of place. Not even a speck of blood. But, I know it's an illusion. Carnage is close by, waiting to surprise me at any given moment.

I make my way into the living room and stop dead in my tracks. Bodies. Dozens of corpses, frozen in petrifying death. They're all positioned throughout the room as if life still flows through their veins. Women fully dressed in ball gowns and cocktail dresses are propped in sitting positions on the couches. A man sits at the grand piano, outfitted in a crisp tuxedo, his pale fingers resting on the keys. People stationed at the bar, their cold, dead hands wrapped around crystal glasses.

The people that work for me, respect me, even care for me. The very ones that relied on me to protect them - all of them a part of a show set up just for me. All of them slaughtered, their eyes

completely opaque, signifying their gruesome death.

Precious life was selfishly sucked out of them. They were probably awake for it all - felt as every one of their internal organs shut down one by one before liquefying. They felt their blood run cold, as their heartbeats stilled. They felt the fire in their lungs, as they took their last breath.

"Beautiful, isn't it?" a voice says from behind me.

I turn around slowly, meeting the sparkling blue eyes of the one person who was supposed to stand by my side, no matter what. The one I thought shared my vision of what this life should be. The one I once called my brother.

"What the fuck have you done?" I sneer.

Varshaun descends the staircase wearing his finest suit, his black hair meticulously slicked back. He's dressed for the occasion as well. Hell, he's made a fucking meal out of this massacre.

"Isn't it obvious, old friend? It's a grand ball! In your honor, no less. Don't tell me you're surprised."

"Surprised? Motherfucker, you're delusional. You've killed everyone - every employee. Every human..."

"Right!" he barks with a clap of his hands. "You're absolutely right! Humans - weak, pathetic, sniveling. They're no better than animals. And I killed them because...because I can. Because *we* can, Niko."

He steps in front of me and grasps my shoulder, his eyes dancing with excitement. "We are gods, brother. Fucking gods. We can do whatever we want. And you know what? I felt like having a little fun. But don't worry; it gets better. I didn't stop there."

I shrug out of his hold and narrow my eyes. "What do you mean?"

"I mean ... I killed them. Not just the humans. I killed them *all*. The guards, your council, even precious Nadia."

"You killed Nadia?" I hiss in disbelief. "You killed my people? *Your* people?"

"Eh," he replies with a wave of his hand. "Collateral damage. I told them not to interfere, but somehow, they've all become just as self-righteous as you."

"Varshaun, you do know the crime you have committed. You do realize I can't, and won't, protect you."

"Protect me?" he laughs, slapping his thigh. "Now why would you need to protect me, when there's no one here to protect you?"

I stare at him, speechless. What has happened to the man I considered my family? Have I been consorting with a deranged stranger this entire time?

"So it's you? The soul-sucker? You're the fucking fiend."

"Ding, ding, ding!" he jibes. "But I wouldn't put a label on it. Let's just say, I've got a hearty appetite, and lately, I've been craving something new. Something soft and sweet. But a little spicy. Maybe with a splash of Voodoo? And you know what would be extra tasty? Laveau blood. Oooh, I haven't had that in decades."

Writhing blue flames instantly snake up my arms at the mention of Amelie's bloodline. I take a step back as a feeling of overwhelming fury washes over me. We, the Dark, may crave fear to get our rocks off, but what really gets us going? What kicks our power into overdrive, making us nearly unstoppable?

Rage. Wrath. It's the ultimate deadly sin.

"Watch your tongue, motherfucker, if you want to keep it," I grit, my jaw tight. Burning frost collects behind my eyes, almost like a bullet in the chamber. I'm ready. If Varshaun thinks he can get to Amelie, he really is off his fucking rocker.

He smiles, looking every bit as sinister as a snake in the Garden of Eden. Blue fire engulfs his own hands, and I notice it's fuller. Denser. Even his eyes shine brighter than ever before. "Well, of course I want to keep it. I'll need it to lick that pretty, pink cunt before I fuck it until it bleeds. And where is our Amelie this evening? She's missing her party."

At the sound of her name on his lips, I growl, causing the ground to shake. Everything rattles around us, emitting a low roar. Crystal glasses and liquor bottles crash to the ground, and the carefully positioned corpses fall over in stiffened heaps. Wind billows the curtains and whips around us, spawning whirlwinds throughout the vast room.

Varshaun looks on in wonder, completely oblivious to his impending ass-kicking. "Bravo, Nikolai! Bravo! It's been so long since I've seen you worked up. I must admit, I was afraid you were losing your edge. Growing soft, if you will. But now… now that the old you is back, how about we go fetch your little French maid and handle her together? We'll fuck her brains out. Fill that pretty little mouth with two cocks. Rip open every tight, little hole and watch her cry and bleed. Then, when we've used her all up, we'll breathe in every drop of that Laveau blood. Send a message to those bottom-feeding vermin."

"No," I growl. My whole body quakes, intensifying the tremors under our feet.

"No? Fine. Suit yourself. I didn't want to share anyway."

He strikes first, launching a ball of white-hot flames at me that I block, but only just so. He's stronger. Stronger as if he had been storing power for weeks. Stronger as if he had killed dozens of our kind.

I attack with my own current, chanting a spell in our native tongue to weaken him. It's useless. My words don't even penetrate him. He's been protected, but I don't even have time to execute a counter-attack before he's rushing me, right through my stream of electric fire, as if it doesn't even hurt him. As if he is impervious to my magic.

"Fuck you!" he grits, tackling me to the ground. He punches me in the face with enough force to decapitate a human. I throw my own powerful blows, aiming for every exposed vulnerable spot.

We roll on the ground, punching, kicking, scratching for survival. The gruesome sounds of ripping flesh and cracking bones are muted by the roar of deadly winds around us. Everything around us shakes, and the floor beneath us cracks open, creating a fissure that runs through the length of the house. A Category 5 hurricane is about to ensue, right here on Bourbon Street. Our blood is not the only that will spill tonight.

Pain and exhaustion seizes my body, and somehow, Varshaun overtakes me. He pins me down, and bares his blood-stained teeth. His hair is wild and matted with the thick, red substance, and he has a deep gash over his eye. I've injured him, but I know I don't look much better.

"I've wanted to kill you for decades, you spoiled little fuck! You don't deserve this power. You don't deserve the crown. You aren't worthy to call yourself Dark!"

"At least I have the crown, you piece of shit. I should have left you in the streets where I found you!" I spit in his face, splattering it with my own blood.

He spreads his palm, and I go limp, my entire body seized with paralysis. *How? How could he possibly...? No. No! This is impossible! No one has this power. No one except ...*

"You see, Little Skotos, I've picked up a few more tricks."

Just like Malcolm when I stifled all function of his body before killing him, I can't move. Shit, I can't even blink. All I can manage is a strangled, unintelligible groan.

"What's that, old friend? You're going to kill me? Aw, how cute, Little Skotos. But I'm sorry to tell you, today is just not your day."

As if right on cue, as if choreographed by the sick fucker himself, Amelie runs into the room, fear and confusion painted on her face. At first, she doesn't see me through the haze of wind and debris, but as soon as our eyes lock, she screams my name, racing to my aid. I try to struggle to get free of the invisible restraints, but I know it's futile. There's nothing I can do to save her. Shit, I can't even save myself.

"Ah, ah, ah. Time for you to have a seat," Varshaun admonishes, halting her advance. With his other hand, he guides her body to the nearest chair, giving her a front row view of the carnage. When he turns back to me, his eyes are nearly white with his lust for magic. "Now that the gang's all here, let's go through this step by step, shall we? First, I'm going to rip your heart out. Then I'm going to fucking eat it."

He whips his head back to Amelie who sits just feet away, trembling uncontrollably. "Then I'm going to take Miss Laveau upstairs to your bed, and stab her with my dick until she bleeds my cum."

I hear his voice, but the words are muffled. I don't give a damn about his threats. All I can see is Amelie. My eyes stay locked on hers and hers on mine. Anguished tears slide down her cheeks, and her teeth chatter in fright. I want to take it all away. I want to kiss away those tears, and make it so she never cries again. I want to hold her close, tuck her under my arm and lay her head on my chest while she dreams of me. I want to show her the world, and all the beauty in it, that would still pale in comparison to her.

I want to love her, even if for the rest of her human days. I never want her to hurt again. Never want her to struggle again. I just want to make her as happy as she has made me in just a matter of weeks.

I want to be better. Better for her. Better for both of us.

Varshaun, long-winded and theatrical as always, even as a demented killer, presses a hand to my chest. I feel the pressure, and I know the end is near. And I will die peacefully, honorably, with Amelie's face the last thing I see.

So quick that I think I'm imagining it, her eyes flash with brilliant gold. I tell myself I am hallucinating with loss of blood, but something remarkable happens. Warmth. All over me. It starts as a slow burn before kindling into a raging fire, thawing my frozen senses.

I know this is no hallucination. This is real. It's magic. It's destiny. *Her* destiny. The reason my Amelie was sent to me.

Distracted with his tirade, Varshaun doesn't even see my hand as it flies up to his throat, cutting off his next words. He still has me pinned, being that I don't have full usage of my power, but now that I have a grip on him, nothing but death will make me let go.

"Your first mistake was thinking you could cheat your way into overpowering me," I growl hoarsely. I squeeze harder, hard enough for his eyes to grow wide with panic. Hard enough to feel the tendons in his neck whine through the strain. "Your second was threatening the woman I love. Your crimes are great and punishable by death, and as your prince, the prince of the Dark, it is my duty to bring you to justice. Now, old friend ... *off with your head."*

I watch his terrified expression as my fingers dig into each side of his neck, cutting through muscle, ligaments and arteries. I feel his wet pulse at my palm, hot liquid spurting down my arm and splattering my face. And when my fingers meet my thumb, and Varshaun's head hangs only by a thread of vertebrae, I snap it like a twig and throw the pieces of his carcass aside, not wanting his filth on me for another second.

Amelie runs to my side, free from the restraints upon his death. "Oh my God, baby. Niko, I'm sorry! I know you told me to drive, and I did, but I couldn't! I couldn't leave you. I had to come back!"

I look up at her and give her a smile, lifting a bloodied hand to cup her cheek. "It's ok. It's ok, baby. You don't have to cry anymore," I rasp, suddenly feeling lethargic and weak.

We both look down to assess my injuries, realizing that I have made no attempt to stand. Blood covers ever inch of my shirt, and I know that a good bit of it is mine. My face feels like it's been filled with lead, growing heavier with every passing second. And inside ... inside, I know that something isn't right. Something that was momentarily overridden by adrenaline.

"Oh no," she cries, gently touching my face. "You're hurt. What can I do? You need help!" She looks around frantically, searching for some sign of life.

"There's no one. Nothing we can do. I'll heal," I assure her. But I know it's a lie. There's no coming back from this. Not without something extra to aid in the process.

"Let me help you." She pulls down the neckline of her sweater, ripping the fabric to fully expose her chest. *"Breathe* me. Let me help you heal."

I shake my head, and instantly cringe. I know I've sustained a serious head injury. "No. No, I won't do that."

"Please! I'll be fine, I promise. It will help you, won't it? Won't it?"

I know I should lie again, but for some reason, with Death looking me square in the face, I can't even find the strength to speak anything but truth. "Yes. It will help."

"Then do it. Please. I love you, Niko, and I'm not going to let you leave me. You promised! You promised you wouldn't leave! Please, just do this for me."

She brings her body down next to mine and positions her throat and chest right at my mouth. "Please," she begs. A single tear slides off her chin and lands on my bloodied lips. And ... my fate is sealed.

I cradle her in my arms, ignoring the excruciating pain shooting up and down my torso. It's ok; it will all be gone soon. First I kiss her neck gently, barely brushing it with my swollen lips. Then my eyelids flutter closed, and I inhale.

I breathe paradise. Bliss. Life.

Golden light flows into my body. I can taste it. Smell it. Hear it. Hell, I become it. Weightless, I float on fluffy clouds to euphoria, where my senses erupt in ecstasy. I'm flying, kissing the sun, feeling warm wind glide over my body. And Amelie is with me. Laughing, smiling, kissing, loving, living, dying...

Dying.

I open my eyes, and grasp her body slumped against mine. She doesn't make a sound, as I gently yet urgently ease her down onto her back. "Amelie! Amelie, baby, talk to me!"

But I know it's too late. Every injury I sustained has been given to her. She took it, took away my pain. She received my death so she could give me life.

I shake her lifeless body, screaming her name over and over. And, by some miracle, she sucks in a shallow breath and barely opens her eyes.

"Amelie, what did you do, baby? What did you do?" Moisture falls from my eyes and runs into my mouth. It's warm and salty. Tears. *My* tears.

"It's ok. It's what's supposed to happen. It's what I was sent for," she whispers.

The tears fall faster and harder, clouding my vision. "No, no, no. But I was supposed to save you! If I loved you, I could save you. And I do, baby. So fucking much. I love you. I'm so sorry. I went too far. Please. You have to live. You have to live for me!"

Amelie smiles, and even though her body is cold, it fills me with warmth. "I have, baby. I've lived for ten years with you."

"No! I don't accept that! That's not enough! If I loved you, I could save you. That's what you said. That's what the fucking Light said, dammit! I love you. So now, I can save you!"

Her frail, trembling hand reaches out to touch my face, and she looks into my eyes, those amber irises captivating me one last time. "It's not me you need to save."

The next moments whirl by like a dream. Colors too bright, distorted, muted. You see it happening, but you can't stop it. You can't jump in and intervene. You can't keep her from taking her last breath. You can't stop her eyelids from closing, sending her into eternal slumber. You can't end the debilitating agony that wracks your entire frame, piercing straight down into your tattered soul, as you helplessly watch her slip away.

I could die a thousand deaths, yet I still would not find peace. It wouldn't make me loathe myself any less for killing her. For trading her warmth for cold stillness. For stealing her light and replacing it with darkness. It still wouldn't bring my Amelie back to me.

I am banished to roam the earth in perpetual night, cursed to lifetime upon lifetime of self-destruction and pain. And that still isn't penance for what I've done. I am a demon, and I have burned. I've watched everything I love crumple into dust and ash. And I'll spend eternity burning in my own personal hell without her here to save me. Just as I should have saved her.

Amelie was my dream. She was my life. My love. My reason to *breathe*.

EPILOGUE

Wind billows in from the east, kissing the Aegean before filtering through the loose fabric of her flowing gown. The beautiful woman stands on her balcony, overlooking the sea, watching the waves crash against the jagged rocks. Sunlight glints off the crystal blue waters, making them sparkle. She loves this view. It has always been her favorite. So many fond memories are tied to that beach. Memories that conjure feelings of joy, happiness and love. Things she hasn't felt in many moons.

"Your Highness, there is news from New Orleans. The task has been completed," a voice says from behind her.

"Good," she replies without turning. "The damage?"

"Moderate. They're spinning it as a tropical storm."

"And Nikolai?"

"He is fine. Distraught, but healthy. On his way home."

"The girl?"

"Dead. All of them, dead. No witnesses, as you requested."

"Good." She fingers a dark, spiraled curl, before tucking it neatly behind her ear. "My sweet, sweet son. One day, he'll see it was for his own good. That it was to protect him. He's too young, too weak to understand that now. Which is why he can never know about this. Do you understand?"

"Yes, ma'am. Also…there is one other thing."

"Go on," the stunning woman sighs with boredom.

"Your son … he's been found."

Delia Skotos spins, a confused scowl marring her perfect features. "What are you talking about, girl? You just said he was coming home, did you not?"

Aurora trembles at the queen's bitter tone. She knows Delia

despises her, yet tolerates her out of sheer necessity. If it weren't for her namesake, Delia would've slaughtered Aurora ages ago.

"Not Nikolai, your highness," she squeaks. "Dorian. They've found him. The Dark prince is back."

ERMAGHERD!!!!

What a sad, horrible ending!

I know you want to throw your book, cry, curse the day I was born or a combination of the three, but please put down the Voodoo doll (that looks nothing like me, by the way) and take a deep breath.

Better?

Ok.

If you've read *Dark Light* & *The Dark Prince*, then you will know that Nikolai is a prequel to Gabriella and Dorian's story. We got to meet Niko in TDP and he made quite the impression. I wanted to write Nikolai because I wanted you all to know him better. To understand where that compassion and underlying pain stems from. Niko suffered greatly at the end of his story, but I assure you, it was absolutely necessary. I'm not a COMPLETE sadist.

No worries, folks. You'll get it in *Light Shadows*. Or you may hate me even more. Guess we'll just have to wait & see...

ACKNOWLEDGMENTS

First & foremost, I want to thank YOU, the readers, for taking a chance on me, and my writing. There are a million titles on Amazon, Barnes & Noble and Kobo, yet, for some reason, you chose mine. Thank you. A thousand times thank you! You have no idea what that means to me.

I want to thank my friends and family for their unconditional love and support throughout my journey with publishing. It's been scary, exciting, frustrating, exhilarating and emotional, and you have been there every step of the way. I could not have done this without you guys. Seriously.

Big thanks to the blogs and reviewers that have pushed the hell out of my books and have been so incredibly gracious with their time and efforts. Y'all are amazing. Simply awesome. I could not have gotten this far without you!

Along this crazy ride, I have met some amazing people. Readers, bloggers and authors that I am now honored to call friends.

Ashley Tkachyk: I love you, babe. I can't even imagine where I'd be without your help and support. Since TDP, you've been such an incredible beta reader & friend. See you soon! We can party with the moose and bears!

Claribel Contreras: We've come a long way, C, and this is only the beginning. Thank you for putting up with my whining and pessimism, and all the corny songs I send you. I can't even describe how much your support means to me. Started from the bottom…lol

Emmy Montes: My sister from another mister…love you, girl! So amazing that after a year, we're still together. And although we may not be living next door like we planned, we'll build our slightly inappropriate bond through memes and raunchy pictures.

Gail McHugh, Madeline Sheehan, Karina Halle, Cindy Brown: Thank you for being amazing women and writers. Especially for putting up with me this long. I've learned so much from each and every one of you. The talks, the advice, the encouragement, the inspiration, the bitch fests, the love fests… Love you all!

My flippin' awesome editor Tracey Buckalew who has had my back through it all. Love you, woman!

Angie McKeon for twisting my arm and forcing me to promote, lol. You rock, babe.

Elle Chardou for swooping in and being awesome when I needed you. You saved my life, girl!

Stephanie White for yet another amazing cover! Three down…

And to everyone who has ever shared, tweeted, commented, posted or simply told someone about my books, this is for YOU. You made this happen. Keep pushing me to give you stories, and I promise, I will do just that.

-S

ABOUT THE AUTHOR

Most known for her starring role in a popular sitcom as a child, S.L. Jennings went on to earn her law degree from Harvard at the young age of 16. While studying for the bar exam and recording her debut hit album, she also won the Nobel Prize for her groundbreaking invention of calorie-free wine. When she isn't conquering the seas in her yacht or flying her Gulfstream, she likes to spin elaborate webs of lies and has even documented a few of these said falsehoods.

Some of S.L.'s devious lies:

FEAR OF FALLING
THE DARK LIGHT SERIES
❖ Dark Light
❖ The Dark Prince
❖ Nikolai (a Dark Light novella)
❖ Light Shadows- *coming soon*
TAINT- *coming in 2014*

Meet the Liar:
www.facebook.com/authorsljennings
Twitter: @MrsSLJ

7984653R00065

Made in the USA
San Bernardino, CA
23 January 2014